THE WITCH OF WITHYFORD

THE WITCH OF WITHYFORD

And Other Stories

GRATIANA CHANTER

Edited and with an introduction by
Gina R. Collia

Published by Nezu Press
Queensgate House,
48 Queen Street,
Exeter, Devon,
EX4 3SR,
United Kingdom.

This edition published 2024

The Witch of Withyford: A Story of Exmoor first published by J. M. Dent & Co., 1896.

ISBN-13: 978-1-7393921-8-5

In the interest of preservation, the punctuation and spelling of the original first edition text have been maintained, and the original formatting has been used wherever possible. Only minor publisher errors and spelling inconsistencies have been silently corrected.

A number of the words and phrases that appear within this work are taken from the Devonshire dialect. Each is translated within a footnote upon its first appearance. As some words and phrases appear more than once, a glossary is provided at the back of this book to avoid the need to seek out previous footnotes to find translations.

CONTENTS

Gratiana Chanter
The Girl's Dream Annual, 1903.

Gratiana Chanter
'A Typical Devon Daughter'
by Gina R. Collia

Gratiana Chanter was born at the vicarage in Ilfracombe, North Devon, on 9 May 1857, the fifth child of Rev. John Mill Chanter (1808-1893) and his wife, Charlotte (née Kingsley, 1827-1882).[1] Charlotte Chanter, fearless fern-hunter and author of *Ferny Combes*, was born in Barnack, Cambridgeshire,[2] to Charles Kingsley (1781-1860) and his wife, Mary (née Lucas, 1787-1873),[3] but she spent the early years of her childhood in Clovelly, forty-odd miles southwest of Ilfracombe, where her father served as curate and then rector.[4] Charlotte's eldest brother, also called Charles Kingsley (1819-1875), was the well-known author of *Westward Ho!* and *The Water-Babies*, and her youngest brother, Henry, was the author of *The Recollections of Geoffry Hamlyn* and *Ravenshoe*.

John Mill Chanter, the third son of Rev. William Chanter (1766-1859) and his wife, Mary (née Wolferstan, 1770-1824), was born at the parsonage in Hartland, Devon,[5] where the scenery is 'grand, marvellous, and awful; the thunder of the Atlantic is for ever in one's ears; the salt spray in one's face, glorious, invigorating, and inspiring'.[6] And it was in Hartland, a next-door neighbour to Clovelly, that John spent his childhood days, in a land 'full of many a wild story of smuggling, wrecking, and the supernatural.'[7] He was appointed vicar of Ilfracombe in April 1836,[8] and on 8 May he 'read himself in'.[9]

The Kingsleys had first made the acquaintance of John Mill Chanter in 1830.[10] During the following years, with the Kingsleys living in Clovelly and John and his family residing in neighbouring

Hartland, it was natural that they should see something of each other. When the Kingsleys left Clovelly for Chelsea in 1836, they continued to visit North Devon when the opportunity arose, and in January 1848 they visited Ilfracombe.[11] Charlotte, then twenty years old, and John, twenty years her senior, had a great deal in common. They shared an intense love of nature and, along with Charlotte's brother Charles, spent a considerable amount of time exploring Ilfracombe and the surrounding areas.

> ' "I remember" (said a dear old friend) "…Miss Kingsley, had a class of girls; I was one of them, and Mr. Charles would often come in when we were there, and make us all laugh with his funny, quaint sayings. Long expeditions they took together, Miss Kingsley, Charles, and the Vicar, mostly on horseback (for they were all at home in the saddle) away to little Trentishoe, or beautiful Lynton and Lynmouth, or the other way to Braunton Burrows, on botanising excursions, or for a long stretching gallop across the yellow sands of

Ilfracombe Town and Harbour, published by Fisher, Son & Co., 1830.

Ilfracombe Vicarage, by Gratiana Chanter, from *Wanderings in North Devon.*

> Woollacombe to Croyde, with the fragrant scent from the brown seaweed in their faces. Pleasant days indeed they must have been." '[12]

The following year, on 10 May 1849, John and Charlotte were married at Clifton Church, Gloucestershire, after which the couple returned to Ilfracombe vicarage, where they would remain together for the next thirty-three years.[13]

Holy Trinity Church, from *Twenty-Four Views of Ilfracombe* by J. Gadsby, c. 1875.

When John Mill Chanter first took on the role of vicar of Ilfracombe, the parish church, Holy Trinity, was in a terrible state; the pews were full of woodworm, the windows rattled in their frames, and the stones along the aisles had been so badly laid that the foul odour from those buried beneath found its way into the church itself.[14] The vicarage and its garden were in as sorry a state as the parish church. The house had been home to countless rodents for years; in fact, the very first soul to greet him when he arrived at his new home was a very large rat.[15] When it rained, the kitchen floor 'used to be an inch or two deep in water, so that the maids were obliged to trot about in pattens.'[16] And the garden was an overgrown wilderness, surrounded by derelict barns. John set to work right away; the barns were removed, 'the rats were dismissed', and he planted every tree and shrub in the vicarage garden himself.[17]

The vicarage was a 'long low house with a buff coloured face and deep finely slated roof, not always even, but gently undulating as if its old beams had wearied with keeping the horizontal for so many centuries, and had lowered their aching arms to a more restful position.'[18] Within the oldest part of the house—above the kitchen, which was thought to have been the original mansion house's entrance hall—there was a haunted room; it was used as a lumber room as all refused to sleep in it.[19] The ghosts were said to be those of two pretty children, murdered by their uncle for their money, who wandered the room and sighed.[20]

The Chanters' first child and only son, Kingsley, was born on 24 March 1850.[21] Mary Geraldine arrived the following year, on 5 June.[22] Then came Louisa Cadogan (15 March 1853),[23] Mabilla (15 November 1854),[24] and Gratiana (9 May 1857).[25] Katherine Stanley was born two years after Gratiana, on 19 February 1859,[26] and the Chanters' final child Charlotte Joyce, arrived four years later, on 28 June 1863.[27]

South Side of Vicarage, by Gratiana Chanter, from *Wanderings in North Devon.*

Since becoming vicar of Ilfracombe, in addition to providing church services, directing the renovation of Holy Trinity, and raising funds for the construction of a new church to serve the town's increasing population, John had held classes at the vicarage for both girls and boys, day and Sunday school classes 'in the tumble-down room over the Market', and he had an infant school at the Quay.[28] He taught the schoolmistress himself, to so high a standard that she satisfied the school inspectors for forty years.[29] And he and Charlotte provided all of their own children with an education; various newspaper reports listed their children's achievements in school examinations.[30]

The vicar's 'quiet humour and power of telling a good story' made him a delightful companion for his children,[31] and Charlotte, who 'had an endless stock of delightful German legends and fairy-tales at her fingers' ends', captivated them with tales of goblins, water nymphs, Devon pixies, and the headless Mullacott Ghost.[32] In 1858, the Chanters' collections of tales for children, *Jack Frost and Betty Snow*, was published by Griffith and Farran. The stories within the small volume, about 'the different dogs, cats, and birds, who had from time to time formed part of their household',[33] were dedicated to Kingsley, who was then eight years old, 'for whom they were written to enliven the weariness of a rainy week'.[34]

Charlotte and John Chanter were keen naturalists, and they encouraged their children to take an interest in the natural world around them. They possessed an adventurous spirit and weren't afraid to get their hands dirty; they enjoyed exploring uncharted territory, and their explorations around the Devonshire countryside often required that they 'rough it'.[35] The people of Ilfracombe were very much aware of the Chanters' great interest in the local flora and fauna, and the vicar was considered 'an authority on such matters'.[36] On one occasion, a gentleman walking on the beach at the Tunnels encountered what he thought was 'a large lump of meat' between some rocks and gave it a poke with his stick. When, in response, the 'impolite mass of blubber' spurted him with water, onlookers suggested a consultation with the vicar of Ilfracombe was in order. John, with the assistance of Rev. J. C. Lewis, performed an examination and pronounced it to be 'a fine young "octopus" '.[37]

Gratiana inherited her parents' passionate love of nature. She also inherited their spirit of adventure. From her mother, 'a brilliant and cultured woman', she inherited her story-telling ability; from her father, great skill with a fishing rod.[38] The vicar was a keen angler; from childhood he had been 'devoted to the gentle art of "fishing." '[39] In adulthood, there was nothing he loved more than to 'wander rod in hand up some moorland valley, enticing the speckled trout from his pebbly nook'.[40] Gratiana's childhood was 'a record of a healthy, happy, out-of-door life', spent wandering about the North Devon countryside, 'up and down the lovely moorland trout streams', with her father, 'one of the most noted fishermen of his day'.[41] She, like her father, was an expert angler and as a child sometimes returned home after a day's fishing with 'a basket of seventy trout'.[42] Many years later, when Gratiana spoke of her childhood to the *Girl's Realm Annual*—of her love of nature, her writing, her drawing and painting, and her ability to cross an Exmoor bog unharmed—she was pronounced 'a typical daughter of Devon'.[43]

Also from her father, Gratiana inherited a love of music; the vicar's family, on his mother's side, were famous for their singing voices,[44] and the vicar himself was president of the Ilfracombe Choral Society from 1875 to 1888.[45] Gratiana, her father, and her sisters—particularly Louisa, who was generally referred to as Lilian or Lily—regularly performed at concerts and amateur theatricals held at Holy Trinity, the town hall, local schools, and the Ilfracombe Battery of the 1st Devon Artillery of Volunteers;[46] Gratiana, being a talented artist, also painted the scenery for some performances.[47]

In October 1868, Gratiana and her family visited Morwenstow,

Tonacombe Manor, from a drawing by J. Ley Pethybridge, c. 1910.

located about ten miles to the south of the vicar's childhood home in Hartland. Gratiana described Tonacombe Manor, the fine medieval house where she and her family stayed, as 'suggestive of everything that was mysterious and delightful.'[48] One of Tonacombe's bedrooms was haunted by a ghost called Zachary, 'a delightful place to creep to in the twilight, and peep through the keyhole, with the expectation of witnessing the ghostly Zachary performing ghostly deeds'.[49] An external stone staircase led from a little courtyard to the haunted chamber.[50] During their visit, there were many storms, and 'miles inland could be heard the raging of the sea… a green black mountain of water, rounding and rolling on, ever gathering in force and size as it nears the bristling shore and boulder-laden beach'.[51] The Chanters spent most of their time on the cliffs or under them, looking for Cornish diamonds.[52]

The following year, when Gratiana was twelve years old, her father bought the Millslade Inn, in the village of Brendon, near Lynton, and converted it into a private residence.[53] The Chanters had stayed at the inn from time to time over the years, to have access to the nearby East Lyn river for trout fishing, and after their purchase of it their summer holidays were always 'passed amongst the wooded vales, and breezy moorlands with which it is surrounded.'[54] They travelled to Millslade in one of Colwill's "three-horse breaks", driving through Ilfracombe, 'with a farewell look at the harbour', and then on to Hele Bay, Watermouth, Combe Martin, Parracombe—where tea was taken at the Fox and Goose[55]—along Dean Steep to Barbrook Mill, then on to Lynton, Countisbury, and finally Brendon.[56] Gratiana described the house as 'not a handsome one, but a comfortable and cosy home, situated in a singularly beautiful position'.[57] The area was, and still is, very popular amongst anglers and artists.

On 2 December 1869, Gratiana's only brother, Kingsley, enlisted in the Merchant Navy. One year later, he deserted.[58] He did not return to England, and Gratiana had not seen her brother for more than five years when, in January 1875, while the vicar was suffering from a severe attack of bronchitis,[59] the Chanters received news that Kingsley was dead.[60] He had been travelling on an American steamer when, having fallen or been washed overboard, he drowned 'in the element he always loved so well'; according to the *Ilfracombe Chronicle*, 'the free-hearted youth', who

Millslade, by Gratiana Chanter, from *Wanderings in North Devon.*

appears to have been well liked, was 'a victim to his too great love of adventure'.[61]

By the time of Kingsley's death, Gratiana's mother was seriously ill. She suffered from chronic myelitis—chronic inflammation of the spinal cord[62]—the common symptoms of which include sensations of numbness or tingling, pain, fatigue, and muscle weakness; at the end of the nineteenth century, chronic myelitis would usually result in complete paralysis and, after a prolonged and painful illness, death.[63] Her physician would have required her to 'keep in a horizontal position' and 'never lie on the back'.[64] Charlotte accompanied her family on a holiday visit to Millslade for the last time in the summer of 1877.[65]

Charlotte Chanter died at Ilfracombe vicarage on 19 March 1882; Gratiana was twenty-four years old at the time.[66] During the morning before Charlotte's burial, which took place five days later, 'the bells of the Parish Church rang out muffled peals', and throughout the town shops were closed and blinds were drawn 'as a token of respect for the deceased lady's memory'.[67] During the funeral service the church was crowded,[68] and a hundred or so of the town's inhabitants attended the burial. She was buried 'amid general manifestation of sorrow' in a vault constructed 'in the new portion of the churchyard' at Holy Trinity.[69]

For the next four years, John Chanter, continued as vicar of Ilfracombe, and he and his daughters remained at Ilfracombe vicarage.[70] However, in November 1886 Edward Henry Bickersteth, the Bishop of Exeter, suggested that John, being then seventy-eight years old, should resign on account of his age.[71] The vicar's parishioners were wholly in favour of him remaining in his post, and it appears that the vicar himself was entirely willing to continue his work, but the bishop favoured retirement. During the first week of December, the vicar tendered his resignation; it was accepted immediately.[72] Before the year was out, the bishop had offered the living of Ilfracombe to John's replacement.[73] A public meeting was held in March 1887 to discuss the collection of subscriptions for a testimonial to the vicar's fifty-one years of faithful service,[74] and in March the following year John was presented with a silver salver and a purse of one hundred guineas.[75] By the beginning of the following year, he and his daughters had left Ilfracombe and moved permanently to Millslade.

In September 1887, Gratiana's memoir of her father, *Wanderings in North Devon: Being Records and Reminiscences in the Life of John Mill Chanter, M. A., Oxon, 51 Years Vicar of Ilfracombe*, was published by Twiss & Son of Ilfracombe. In addition to providing a vivid picture of her father's life, and of her own childhood, Gratiana produced a number of drawings to illustrate the book.[76] 'The whole volume,' wrote the 'local literature' reporter for the *North Devon Journal*, 'teems with scenes, stories and occurrences which have an inexhaustible interest for the people of North Devon' and for the tourists who 'flock hither in the summer's prime.'[77]

Rev. John Mill Chanter, 1887, from *Wanderings in North Devon.*

John Mill Chanter died at Millslade at the age of eighty-four on 11 February 1893.[78] The night before his funeral, his body was taken from Brendon to Ilfracombe, 'escorted by an immense crowd', and his coffin remained in Holy Trinity's chancel overnight, watched over by devoted members of the late vicar's congregation.[79] Shortly before his funeral, which was attended by about 1,300 mourners, the bells rang a muffled peal.[80] He was laid to rest alongside his late wife on 16 February.[81] The following year, a new lych gate was erected at Holy Trinity as a memorial to the late vicar; the dedication ceremony took place on 18 October 1894.[82]

By the time of the vicar's death, Gratiana's eldest sister, Mary, and her youngest, Charlotte, had become Sisters of Mercy,[83] and Lily had married Rev. James Frederic Vallings and was living in Hampshire.[84] Only Gratiana, Mabilla and Katherine remained at Millslade. The three sisters took an active interest in their local community and were 'always ready to help in any entertainment for the benefit of the parish'; they undertook sole management of the Brendon Men's Club, and they regularly took part in concerts that were held at the local schoolroom in aid of that institution.[85]

The lych gate dedicated to the memory of John Mill Chanter.

In November 1892, various periodicals carried a short notice that Gratiana planned to publish a book (or booklet) about R. D. Blackmore's *Lorna Doone: A Romance of Exmoor*. She had 'made a study of the traditions and facts of the book', and planned to 'embody the results of her researches' in *The Forty Thieves of Exmoor; Or, The Doones of Badgworthy*.[86] She did indeed publish such a work in 1898—it was printed by Suckling & Co. of Garrick Street—but I have been unable to locate a copy.[87] Four years earlier, however, a short autobiographical story appeared in the *Auckland Star* entitled 'The Forty Thieves of Exmoor; or, The Doones of Badgworthy: The Author's Childhood in the Doone Valley, and Traditions Told Her'.[88] During the same year, she contributed a ballad, 'The Lady of Sevilla', to *Popular British Ballads: Ancient and Modern*.[89]

Gratiana's novella *The Witch of Withyford: A Story of Exmoor*, containing her own illustrations, was published by J. M. Dent & Co. in May 1896. In it, Nance Darvel, a gruesome woman who lives in a hovel, is intent on punishing a slight by destroying the life of the local squire. It is an uncanny tale of witchcraft, superstition, child-theft and revenge, set in Gratiana's beloved Devonshire and told by an elderly servant of Withyford Grange. The *Pall Mall Gazette* described it as:

> 'The prettiest little book, in the daintiest binding, written in clear, delicate style and with only sufficient dialect to add piquancy to the narrative of the old servant of the Grange. The story breathes of the sweet Devon air, and is full of quaint folklore, and old world loyalty and simplicity, and the beauties of Tor and Combe are vividly described.'[90]

On 14 October 1896, Gratiana married Edward William Longworth Knocker at Brendon Church; she was thirty-nine years old at the time, and Edward was fifteen years her junior.[91] Edward was born in Dover on 3 September 1872, the eldest son of Edward Knocker (1805-1884) and Canadian born Jane Celia Bayly Longworth Dames (1840-1884).[92] Three days after their wedding, Gratiana and Edward sailed from Plymouth to Naples on R. M. S. *Ophir*, a vessel renowned for its opulent interiors that went on to serve as the royal yacht.[93] They spent the first two years of their marriage in Italy, where Gratiana painted a great deal,[94] returning to Millslade in 1898. On 1 August of that year, Mabilla Chanter married Edward Western, a schoolmaster,[95] and following her honeymoon she left Brendon and moved to her husband's home in Dunster. Gratiana and Edward settled down to life at Millslade with Katherine.

While Gratiana was living in Italy, Twiss & Son, the local publisher of *Wanderings in North Devon*, included one of her drawings, a sketch of Holy Trinity Church, in their *Illustrated Guide to Ilfracombe and North Devon* (see page opposite).[96] It is likely, given the number of travel books being produced at the time, that her drawings appeared in other guides to Ilfracombe.[97]

Church of St. Brendan in the village of Brendon.

Holy Trinity, by Gratiana Chanter, from *Illustrated Guide to Ilfracombe.*

In September 1901, *The Rainbow Garden and Other Stories*, a collection of eight 'graceful short stories for children',[98] illustrated by the author and written with 'a touch of pathos and mystery which will appeal to little folk',[99] was published by R. Brimley Johnson.[100] The critic for the *Westminster Review* wrote:

> 'Mr. Brimley Johnson has published a volume of delightful short stories… The tales have all the charm of fairy stories, and there is a thread of exquisite fancy running through them. Perhaps the melancholy note predominates too much in these little stories, which are apparently intended for children… But the writer of this volume of tales has certainly the gift of

> touching the heart… though she writes in a strain of almost unbroken sadness.'[101]

It certainly is true that all of the stories have a melancholy air about them; in all but one, someone or something dies: children, flowers, bees, trees, a windmill… and even a year. But all of the tales in this extremely rare volume are enjoyable.

In 1806, Gratiana contributed one chapter to *The Book of Capri,* entitled 'Some Capri Flowers, and Where They Grow', which was written from her personal experiences of flower-hunting on the island, in the hope that her readers may 'linger long in Capri, and be happy amongst its flowers.'[102] Gratiana had visited Capri for the first time in 1896, when she and Edward stayed at the Hotel Paradiso; she went looking for holly to decorate their hotel room on Christmas Eve but had to make do with a bundle of myrtle and rosemary branches.[103]

In May 1908, Millslade, and the surrounding eleven acres of land, was sold at auction; the furnishings were sold a month later.[104] Katherine went to live with Mabilla and her husband in Minehead,[105] and Gratiana and Edward returned to Italy, where they remained for the rest of their lives; they lived in Pozzuoli in Naples, where Edward was employed by the Armstrong Works, then Rome, where he worked at the Department of the Commercial Counsellor at the British Embassy.[106]

Trebetherick, a tale of shipwrecks, wreckers, hidden treasure, abducted maidens, murder and other evil doings, was published in 1913 by Francesco Giannini & Figli of Naples. The story is told from the perspective of David Rounsevall of Trebetherick in the Parish of St. Enodoc, Cornwall, and begins the night he first hears ghostly Tregeagle howl during a ferocious storm. The reviewer for the *Birmingham Post* wrote:

> '...the whole story is filled with the authentic atmosphere of the West country. It is not only that the "local colour" is plentiful and vivid; all the rest is in keeping. None but a West-country woman could have written it. And one cannot but feel that if her story is to enjoy its deserts it will have to become a classic of the Cornish book-stalls.'[107]

Trebetherick is a real place, thirty-five or so miles south of Morwenstow, and is located, as the story tells us, halfway 'between the Church of St. Enodoc and the hamlet of Polseth' (Polzeath). The church, famous for having been almost buried in sand until the second half of the nineteenth century, is the burial place of John Betjeman, who spent the last years of his life in the village of Trebetherick.[108] The Rounsevalls were also real, though whether or not they ever heard Tregeagle howl we shall never know.

When writing *Trebetherick*, Gratiana appears to have been inspired by actual events which took place in North Devon in 1842. She wrote in *Wanderings in North Devon*:

> 'In old days the evil practice of "wrecking" was carried on to a terrible extent all along the coast. One method of enticing vessels ashore, was to place lights in different spots along the cliffs. If the vessel was a foreigner, or without a pilot, it would often make for the light, the crew thinking it was placed there to guide them in.'[109]

She then described the wrecking of the *William Wilberforce* at Lee, a few miles from Ilfracombe, to demonstrate the villainy which wreckers were capable of. The legend goes that a donkey with a lantern tied to its tail was used to lure the ship onto the rocks; 'the action of the donkey on the beach caused the lantern to move up and down, just as a shiplight would by the action of the waves', leading those aboard the ship to believe they were heading for the safety of Ilfracombe harbour.[110]

The *William Wilberforce* was indeed wrecked at Lee during a heavy gale on 23 October 1842, at about seven o'clock in the evening, and all seven hands were lost.[111] Whether or not the vessel was lured onto the rocks by wreckers looking to loot her, with or without the aid of a donkey, William Huxtable, the Receiver General of Droits of Admiralty and sub-agent to Lloyds, was taking no chances; with the assistance of the Coast Guard Services, he stripped the ship of her sails and rigging immediately, then took possession of her cargo and removed her yards, topmasts, etc., the following day.[112]

Trebetherick was Gratiana's last published work. Edward died on 7 May 1933; he was sixty years old. Gratiana died the following year, on 24 November 1934, at the age of seventy-seven,[113] leaving her estate to her youngest sister, Charlotte Joyce. Gratiana and Edward were buried in the Campo Cestio, the non-Catholic cemetery, in Rome.[114]

Notes

1 For the date: birth certificate, district of Ilfracombe, registered 8 June 1857. Name listed as 'Graciana' (the spelling was altered to 'Gratiana' by 1881: see the *1881 England Census*, Norfolk, Kettlestone); she was also referred to as Grace. For the location: 'Girls That the Counties Are Proud Of', *The Girl's Realm Annual*, 1903, p. 831.

2 *Ferny Combes: A Ramble After Ferns in the Glens and Valleys of Devonshire*, was published by Lovell Reeve in 1856. Barnack is a village and civil parish in the Peterborough unitary authority of the ceremonial county of Cambridgeshire.

3 *Engand, Select Births and Christenings, 1538-1975*. Charlotte was baptised on 17 October 1828. There were seven children in all. The Kingsley's fifth child, Louisa Mary, died in infancy on 14 May 1824, four years before Charlotte's birth: *Stamford Mercury*, 21 May 1824, p. 3.

4 Lady Susan Chitty, *Charles Kingsley's Landscape: His Letters and Memories of His Life*. Newton Abbot: David & Charles, 1976, p. 8. Charles Kingsley served as curate from 1831, then rector from 1832 to 1836.

5 Gratiana Chanter, *Wanderings in North Devon: Being Records and Reminiscences in the Life of John Mill Chanter, M. A., Oxon, 51 Years Vicar of Ilfracombe*. Ilfracombe: Twiss & Son, 1887, p. 1.

6 Ibid., p. 3.

7 Ibid.

8 *Oxford University and City Herald*, 30 April 1836, p. 3.

9 Chanter, op. cit., p. 15.

10 Chanter, op. cit., p. 19.

11 Chitty, op. cit., p. 116.

12 Chanter, op. cit., p. 20.

13 *Bristol, England, Church of England Marriages and Banns, 1754-1938*, Clifton, St. Andrew, Gloucestershire.

14 Chanter, op. cit., pp. 15-16.

15 Ibid., p. 39.

16 Ibid. Pattens: wooden clogs or overshoes that elevate the foot to aid the wearer when walking on wet or muddy ground.

17 Ibid.

18 Ibid.

19 Chanter, op. cit., p. 38.

20 Ibid., p. 43.

21 *Lady's Newspaper and Pictorial Times*, 6 April 1850, p. 30.

22 *Western Times*, 14 June 1851, p. 4.

23 *North Devon Journal*, 17 March, p. 5.

24 *North Devon Journal*, 23 November 1854, p. 8.

25 *Italy, Find a Grave Index, 1800s-Present.*

26 *North Devon Journal*, 24 February 1859, p. 8.

27 *North Devon Journal*, 9 July 1863, p. 8.

28 Chanter, op. cit., pp. 33-34.

29 Ibid., p. 34.

30 *Ilfracombe Chronicle* included school examination results for 'light. heat, electricity' (physics), geography, geometry, and drawing, etc.

31 Chanter, op. cit., p. 40.

32 Ibid., p. 41.

33 Ibid., p. 40.

34 *Jack Frost and Betty Snow: With Other Tales for Wintry Nights and Rainy Days.* London: Griffith and Farran, 1858.

35 Chanter, op. cit., p. 49.

36 *North Devon Journal*, 18 September 1873, p. 8.

37 Ibid. Te octopus was taken to Rev. Lewis's aquarium and was 'alive and well' at the time of the news report.

38 'Girls That the Counties Are Proud Of', in *The Girl's Realm Annual*, 1903, p. 831.

39 Chanter, op. cit., p. 5.

40 Ibid., p. 6.

41 *The Girl's Realm Annual*, op., cit., p. 831.

42 Ibid.

43 Ibid.

44 Chanter, op. cit., p. 9.

45 *North Devon Journal*, 27 May 1875, p. 8 and *Ilfracombe Chronicle*, 12 May 1888, p. 5.

46 *Ilfracombe Chronicle*: 31 March 1883, p. 2 (Devon Artillery); 4 April 1885, p. 2 (Holy Trinity); 9 January 1886, p. 5 Girls' Schoolroom); 24 January 1874, p. 4 (town hall).

47 *Ilfracombe Chronicle*, 9 January 1886, p. 5.

48 Chanter, op. cit., p. 56.

49 Ibid., pp. 57-58.

50 Charles Edward Byles, *The Life and Letters of R. S. Hawker (Sometime Vicar of Morwenstow)*. London: John Lane. p. 617.

51 Ibid., p. 58.

52 Ibid., p. 59.

53 The auction was held on 25 June 1869 at the Golden Lion Hotel, Barnstaple. See *North Devon Journal*, 17 June 1869, p. 1.

54 Chanter, op. cit., p. 64.

55 There has been an inn on the site of the Fox and Goose since the 16th century. The one referred to by Gratiana burned down in 1892; the current Fox and Goose was built in 1894 (*The Historic Environment Record for Exmoor National Park*, MEM23816).

56 Chanter, op. cit., pp. 73-76.

57 Ibid., p. 77.

58 *UK, Apprentices Indentured in Merchant Navy, 1824-1910.* He was in Newcastle, New South Wales, Australia, when he deserted.

59 *Ilfracombe Chronicle*, 5 December 1974, p. 5.

60 *Ilfracombe Chronicle*, 23 January 1875, p. 5. He died on 1 August 1874 according to *England & Wales, National Probate Calendar (Index of Wills and Administrations), 1858-1995).*

61 *Ilfracombe Chronicle*, 23 January 1875, p. 5.

62 Death certificate, district of Ilfracombe, county of Devon, registered 22 March 1882. Causes of death: chronic myelitis and lardaceous disease of the liver (now known as amyloidosis).

63 Byrom Bramwell, M. D., F. R. C. P. (Edin.). *Diseases of the Spinal Cord.* Second edition. Edinburgh: Young J. Pentland, 1884, p. 250.

64 John King, M. D., *The Causes, Symptoms, Diagnosis, Pathology and Treatment of Chronic Diseases.* Cincinnati: Moore, Wilstach & Baldwin, 1867, p. 188.

65 *Ilfracombe Chrinicle*, 11 August 1877, p. 5.

66 UK and Ireland, Find a Grave Index, 1300s-Current.

67 Death certificate.

68 *North Devon Journal*, 30 March 1882, p. 8.

69 Ibid.

70 Lily Chanter had married Rev. James F. Vallings on 20 August 1882; Mary, Mabilla, Gratiana, Katherine and Charlotte Joyce remained living with their father.

71 *Ilfracombe Chronicle*, 13 November 1886, p. 5.

72 *Ilfracombe Chronicle*, 11 December 1886, p. 5.

73 *North Devon Gazette*, 4 January 1887, p. 5.

74 *Ilfracombe Chronicle*, 2 April 1887, p. 3.

75 *Ilfracombe Chronicle*, 10 March 1888, p. 5.

76 Although Gratiana is listed as being the book's editor, the contents would appear to have been written by her, based on stories and information provided by her father. The second half of the book contains a selection of the vicar's sermons.

77 *North Devon Journal*, 22 September 1887, p. 2.

78 *England & Wales, National Probate Calendar (Index of Wills and Administrations), 1858-1995.*

79 *North Devon Journal*, 23 February 1893, p.8.

80 Ibid.

81 Ibid.

82 North Devon Journal, 25 October 1894, p. 3. The lych gate still exists and is a grade II listed building.

83 *North Devon Journal*, 23 February 1893, p.8. Mary Geraldine (known as Sister Geraldine, *1911 England Census*) and Charlotte Joyce (known as Sister Joyce, *1881 England Census*) were members of the Community of St. John Baptist, Clewer, an Anglican religious order of Augustinian nuns. Charlotte Joyce later became a sister of the Community of the Holy Name (*1911 England Census*).

84 *1891 England Census.*

85 *North Devon Journal*, 22 October 1891, p. 3.

86 *The Critic*, 17 December 1892, p. 349.

87 The work was advertised in the *Bookseller*, 6 May 1898, p. 77.

88 *Auckland Star*, 21 April 1894, p. 3.

89 Reginald Brimley Johnson, *Popular British Ballads: Ancient and Modern.* Volume 4. London: J. M. Dent & Co., 1894, pp. 152-154.

90 *Pall Mall Gazette*, 9 May 1896, p. 3.

91 *North Devon Journal*, 22 October 1896, p. 3 and *Devon, England, Church of England Marriages and Banns, 1754-1920.*

92 *Kentish Gazette*, 10 September 1872, p. 5. Edward was the eldest son of Edward and Jane Knocker. However, his father had been married twice before, with issue.

93 *UK and Ireland, Outward Passenger Lists, 1890-1960.*

94 *The Girl's Realm Annual*, op., cit., p. 831.

95 *Exeter and Plymouth Gazette*, 9 August 1898, p. 6.

96 No publication date, but the date included on a railway timetable within it suggests it was published in 1897.

97 As the names of the artists who provided illustrations for these tourist volumes are generally omitted, it would be necessary to compare Gratiana's known work with specific guide books.

98 *Bookseller*, 25 December 1901, p. 96.

99 *London Quarterly Review*, January 1902, p. 198.

100 *Westminster Gazette*, 21 September 1901, p. 8.

101 *Westminster Review*, November, 1901, pp. 593-594.

102 Harold E. Trower, *The Book of Capri.* Naples: Emil Brass, 1906, p. 301.

103 Ibid., p. 292.

104 *North Devon Journal*, 28 May 1908, p. 2.

105 *1911 England Census.*

106 Edward worked for The Armstrong Works, Pozzuoli-Cantiere, in 1918-1919, and he and Gratiana lived at Villa Suigi, Oriano, Pozzuoli, see *Over-Seas Club and Patriotic League: List of Subscribing Members, 1918-1919*, p. 105. p. 105 and *1919-1920*, p. 64. He worked at the British Embassy in Rome toward the end of his life and was awarded an O. B. E., see *The London Gazette*, 2 January 1933, p. 11. The couple lived at 22 Via Aipi in Rome at the time of their deaths, see *England & Wales, National Probate Calendar (Index of Wills and Administrations), 1858-1995*, 1933 and 1935.

107 *Birmingham Daily Post*, 20 May 1914, p. 4.

108 By the 1850s the local clergyman had to be lowered into the church via the skylight in the north transept to perform services (official list entry at Historic England, no. 1211902).

109 Chanter, op. cit., p. 69

110 Chanter, op. cit., pp. 69-70

111 *North Devon Journal*, 3 November 1842, p. 3, and *London Evening Standard*, 29 October 1842, p. 3.

112 *London Evening Standard*, 29 October 1842, p. 3. The figurehead of the William Wilberforce—an representation of the man himself—is now housed within the Cutty Sark's collection of Merchant Navy ships' figureheads, in Greenwich, London.

113 *England & Wales, National Probate Calendar (Index of Wills and Administrations), 1858-1995*, 1933 and 1935.

114 *Italy, Find a Grace Index, 1800s-Current.*

THE WITCH OF WITHYFORD

The Flood in Witches' Combe, by Gratiana Chanter.

CHAPTER I

THE DANCE OF THE WITCH LIGHTS

AND sure as I be a living woman, 'tis the truth I'm going to tell ye, and naught but truth, and there's no person to Withyford as could tell so much about the Grange ways, and the Grange folk: for father he were huntsman to the old Squire for nigh forty year, and mother she looked after the maidens both fore and since the poor lady's death, and you may depend as there was little that passed in the great house as mother didn't know.

The old Squire stayed single till close on forty-one, seeming content with his hounds and hunting and such like; being out on the forest from morn till night with father, and that poor mazed creature, Tom Fool.[1] Sure! the Squire was a hearty soul, dear man! and well set up, and that masterful, that no person dare go against him; not that folks wanted to, he being the Squire, and a proper gentleman. Sure there weren't a soul to Withyford as didn't love him as their own. Even Jack Headen, it wasn't much that he said when Squire he thrashed him within an inch of his life, for taking the stick to Mal. 'Twas knowing the Squire was the Squire, I reckon, and the right man to do it.

'Twas one fine day, so mother saith, the master set off to London to see his sister, and father went with him so far as Exeter to bring back the horses.[2] He bided away a good spell, and sure when at last he came back, he brought his lady along with

---

[1] Mazed: mad, daft, stupid.

[2] Saith: said.

him.[3] I never saw her myself, but from what mother saith, I don't suppose that a more lovely creature ever stepped earth than the mistress, as for her eyes alone, no person could ever forget them, and as for the Squire, he just worshipped her as an angel sent down from heaven.

They'd been man and wife nigh eighteen months when the little maid was born, and Squire (if could be) was more proud of his lady than ever, and there was nought in heaven or earth as he wouldn't have risked his very life to get her, had she wished for it.

Outside the door, crouched right up in a corner, sat that poor mazed critter, Tom Fool, and slinking to one side as a whipped dog, when Nance Darvel the nurse went in or out, for he never could abide her. The Lord alone knows how much that poor fool knew, and how much he didn't.

'Twas not more than two weeks after the little maid was born, when Squire told father he'd hunt with hounds. There'd been an old fox that had carried off a splendid brood of Farmer Jan's chicks, and it weren't the first time as he had done it neither, and Farmer Jan, he was in a pretty way about it, for 'tis a proper trial when you've reared up chicks, to get them sneaked off like that there, and Farmer he thought, the sooner the old fox had gone dead, the better for he.

So the mistress, dear soul! she wouldn't rest till the master he'd got on his scarlet and boots (and my! how proud she looked to see him in them too) and he'd ridden off through the grey Grange gates, with the hounds well in behind him.

Mother saw him stoop to kiss her, afore he went. "Good-bye, my queen, my sweet," he saith, bending down so gentle.

"Good-bye, my lord, my love," she answered back, looking

[3] Bided: stayed, remained.

up so proud with the little maid in her arms. He bent down again and kissed the child, and left the room softly with a blessed look in his eyes.

And Nance Darvel, the nurse, she shut the door behind him.

Many and many's the times that I've heard father speak of that time, so I can tell it word for word, same as he spake it to me.

It was one of these here stillish days, that come in the fall of the year. The beech-trees up to the Grange had turned all colours and the ashes down by the pond had let their leaves go through the frost, though that day the air was a bit misty and full of the smell of autumn.

There were three others along with them, besides father and Squire, Farmer Jan up to Bartin, Farmer Will to Warren, and to be sure, mazed Tom on Jo, for he must needs go where the master went.

The old fox was a sharp one, for they lost him after all, and it came on dimpsey afore they knew how late 'twas, and it weren't no good to try any more.[4] So Farmer Jan and Farmer Will wished them good-night, and rode back over the top of the Combe, for iron chains wouldn't have dragged them Squire's way so late at night, no nor in daylight neither, for he made up his mind to the short cut through "Witches' Combe" to the Grange.[5] 'Twas a cursed road, as no Withyford man ever trod unless he could find no other.

Sure father tried to stop him all he could, for 'twas an oozy nasty place for the horses, if nought else; but Lord! he'd set his mind upon it, and who was father to keep him? and he could see as the Squire was in a fidget to get back to the mistress.

---

4 Dimpsey: twilight, also dim or dark.

5 Combe: a steep, short valley running up from the sea.

So father and mazed Tom, with the hounds well in, followed him down the Combe.

"Never, in all his days," father saith, "had he seen the place look nastier."

Every step they took down, the moor rose higher and blacker above them, shutting out the little light there was. Down, down they went into the black bottom, with a cold smell of rottenness and death a filling of their nostrils. The hounds dropped their tails, and slunk along, scared, as father'd never known them to afore, sure 'twas terrible wist.[6]

They hadn't gone half-way down Cleve, fore father said they see'd a sight as made his hair rise right up on his head, and the sweat run off his face, as he'd mowed a four-acre field, without so much as whetting of his scythe.[7] Sure he must have been in a terrible sweat, and no wonder!

Tom gave a bawl as a screech-owl, and burrowed his head in the heath, like a scared rabbit, while the Squire sat straight and stiff, with his face like a dead man's; his mare's sides frothing white, like beer at brewing time.[8]

Sure! and no wonder! for 'twas sight enough to scare any living man, and drive him mazed for ever.

Down in the bottom they were dancing with lights in their hands, how many they were, nor who they were, father he couldn't rightly say, for being so scared; but he reckoned 'twas the devil's own daughters, and no other, a-dancing their sinful dance, with the

---

6 Wist: haunted or pixie-led (a place where you are likely to be led astray by pixies).

7 Cleve: a cliff, the steep side of a hill.

8 Heath: heather.

smell of death in the air; there might a been five, or there might a been a score; back and fore they danced, in and out, and up and down the combe, for all the world like folks in their shrouds, with candles in their hands, some deathly blue, some white, up and down, like yellow hammers over a hedgerow.

How long they bided there, father never could say, they was just frozed with fear, and dread of they things below. Sudden the wind blew off the moor, and the lights they ran before it, then a shoulder of dark heath came between them, and the combe looked black as hell.

The Squire spoke something low in his teeth, but low as it was, father he caught the words he said, or sure 'twas the prayer he prayed.

"God in heaven, take care of my lady." And his voice trembled as the leaves on the poplar trees down by the churchyard gate.

"Ride man! ride!" he shouted in a hoarse kind of scream, so strange as father scarce felt as 'twas the master as spoke.

"Ride man! ride! as if hell, the devil, and death be at your heels. Ride! ride!"

Lord! 'twas a ride sure enough! father never could tell how they got to Grange gates, for they rode through the Witches' Combe at a hand gallop, with the night as black as ink; a ride no mortal had took afore, or, I reckon, will take again.

They was racing death; and the beasts knew it, and plunged along, through bogs and rocks, as if the devil were behind them, the hounds knew it too, for they kept their noses down, as if they were running a fox, only they ran SILENT. 'Twas the black night above, the black combe below, and no sounds, but the rattle and ring of iron hoofs against the loose stones, the panting and rush of half-mazed horses, and the creakings of the saddle leather.

The lights had danced over the track towards the Grange, and there was three living men as see'd them, and three men as knew what they meant, nought but death, to be sure, to the folks they went to visit.

The Squire was the first through the grey gates, and the first to fling himself off (more dead than alive), and in at the open door, where mother stood waiting for him.

And the hounds ran silent till they reached the Grange yard, and then they flinged their muzzles up and howled, and howled, and howled till the cold dawn crept across the murky sky.

CHAPTER II

OF THE EVIL DOINGS OF NANCE DARVEL

NO person can tell what a day may bring forth; and sure 'tis a true saying, and a blessed one to my thinking, for if we did, most folk would be afeared to face what was coming, and the Lord alone knows what cowards 'twould make of us? Mother'd been down that same afternoon to see the old Jane Bowden, who'd been dreadful bad in her chest a long while back, and scarce could fetch up her breath to breathie.

Mother'd made her a drop of broth, which she fancied might do her good and go down easy like; for the poor old critter was too ill to do such things for herself, being mostly tied to her bed. But mother'd a good heart, and if ever she could do anything for any person you may depend upon it she would.

Her'd set things straight to Grange, and kept Liz to look after the fire, and do any little thing as Nance Darvel wanted, so she didn't feel in any great hurry to get home.

She sat telling with the old Jane a good two hours, for 'twas getting dimpsey when she started up hill to Grange, and that she took easy as she was getting a bit stoutish, and it made her bad to hurry.[9] She went into the hall door, as the kitchen way was a bit further round, when she heard screaming and crying in the mistress's room upstairs, that terrible that her heart stood still in her body and her blood ran properly cold.

Then the mistress's door open and shut, and Nance Darvel stood to the top of the stairs looking down to mother.

---

[9] Telling: talking.

"Lord in heaven! what be the matter?" mother her saith.

" 'Tis the mistress be raving mad," Nance answered slow and cool, "and her'll be a dead woman in her shroud fore morning, sure as my name's Nance Darvel."

Then she wait a bit, and saith slow, "and the baby's gone."

"Dead!" mother screamed.

"Don't screech, you fool!" her saith, "dead! no, not as I know by. But gone, clean gone: I can't tell ye where, not in this house I know, for I've looked."

"Lord, Lord!" mother saith, "now what can you mean, Nance Darvel, for 'taint for a mite of two weeks old to walk out of the door by itself. Some person must have carried it, that's certain."

Mother's head seemed all to a whirly with what Nance Darvel'd a said.

After the little maid, her first thoughts were the *master*. She looked up to where Nance stood calm and quiet above her. But she felt as one turned to stone, and a strange feeling come creeping all over her. She tried to think what was best to do, but sure she could see naught but Nance Darvel's green eyes a staring and a staring, like a cat's in a coal cellar, and sudden she could mind no more, but dropped down like a log at the foot of the stairs where she stood.[10]

'Twas a long time afore she come to, and the sense of what Nance Darvel said came back to her. But soon as it did, and her legs got steady under her, she made all haste to the lady's room, and sure! it near broke her heart when she got there, for she saw as Nance Darvel had spoken the truth, and the lady'd be gone before morn.

She sent Liz down village to tell the folk to search every place they could think of, for the little maid that was lost. And she herself

[10] Mind: remember.

went all over the house from garret to cellar. Lord! what was the use to look, for who could have hidden the maid; who was there she thought to Withyford as would play tricks with ought of the master's, never a soul: where was the blessed lamb? what could it all mean? dear! dear! Lord help her! How could she tell the master?

'Twas then that she heard them all come clackering into the yard, and she prayed the Lord to give her strength and went right out to meet him.[11]

The fire was bright in the hall for she'd set it blazing with good ash logs, thinking to make it cheerful against the time he came; but when the dogs set a howling 'tweren't no good to keep the feel of death from the house any more. It was there, and she knew it.

Master he reeled into the light as a drunken man; that dazed and white-faced, that mother knew he'd had a "warning." He stood there swaying in his boots, while the sweat stood in great beads upon his face and forehead, and he trembled from head to foot.

Mother's heart bled for him; but her just took him by the hand and coaxed him like a child, a liberty she never would have taken, only 'twas life and death, and a body don't stop to think of persons then, for at such times poor folk and gentry seem all alike.

"What is it! what is it! Thirza," he saith. "Tell me the worst, oh! woman! and God help me through with it."

So mother she told him, poor soul, as soft as she could, but he gave one terrible groan as a man in mortal pain, then rose from his chair and climbed the stairs to the mistress's room. Ah Lord! 'twas a different man to the one who but left it that morn.

And sure that night the lady died, and sure that night the master's hair turned white as the snow in January, which but the

11 Clackering: clattering

day before had been black as ripened sloans, and trouble was at his heart, and trouble was in his eyes, and the grief that was upon him seemed greater than he could bear, a burden as seemed to weigh him down, till he almost broke beneath it.[12] Till sudden he raised himself up, and saith, "Thirza! where be the child?"

Mother'd been waiting. She had seen the greater grief had left no room for the smaller, but she knew that the time must come, so she told him soft again, though it wrung her heart to do it.

He sent for them everyone, for every soul in the village. His voice spoke clear and firm, but his eyes looked wild with woe. All came into the hall, every blessed critter, most had been out hunting all night, and I reckon there weren't a combe, nor a hedge, nor a linhay as they hadn't turned out nor looked to.[13] But there weren't a sign of the child inside Withyford nor out of it, except 'twas to bottom of the river, and Lord! who was there to put it there?

So all the folk was there, even to Granfer Lock, nigh gone eighty-four, and he in bed the day before with gout in his feet, so much he knew about it, but he'd got his crutches along with him, for he must know all, and bless you, there's some folk so terrible inquisitive, they'd come out of their very graves to hear a bit of news, and Granfer Lock, well, he was one of they.

So I suppose you may say that all Withyford was there, excepting "mazed Tom," who'd gone off no person knew where, soon as he'd seen the master come out of the mistress's room, though no one took any account of it, as he was ever queer in his ways.

Mother she tried to turn the master from seeing the folk so soon. There was a stuck look in his eyes as she didn't like to see.

---

12 Sloans: Sloe berries, from the *Prunus spinosa.*

13 Linhay: a type of open-fronted farm building.

But he hit the table hard when she spoke till all the glasses jingled, though 'twas solid oak and not an easy one to shake.

"I'll track that damned fiend myself, Thirza," he cried, "and heaven have mercy on him, for I swear as I'll have none. Don't interfere with me, woman, but go, and let me be."

So she let him be, and prayed the Lord as no harm would come of it. Though she greatly feared he was trying himself too much.

So the Squire he sat himself down in the great chair at the top of the hall, still in his scarlet and mud-splashed boots, dear soul! (for he'd taken no thought to changing them), and he had the folk up one by one, and questioned them sharp and clear, same as they do, I've heard tell, in the court of justice up to Exeter.

Most of the women folk were crying soft, out of respect to the master's trouble, and to think he should have to sit there telling, with his lady lying dead upstairs. I don't suppose as there was one in the room as wouldn't have laid down willing, and let him walk right over him, if by so doing 'twould have brought him any comfort. And as for doing him harm or hurt, why mother said she'd have taken her solemn oath on the Bible for every blessed man of them, and not been afeared of judgment.

No person to Withyford had done the deed she was certain. But it always took mother a terrible time to see through any wickedness.

One by one he had them up, no, not one did he let go, till at last it was only Liz and Nance Darvel that was left.

Liz came up crying awful. Mother told her pretty sharp to stop, and not make such a fool of herself (though she really believed the maid had got so far that she couldn't). Fearing 'twould worry the master, she gave her a glass of water, and then Liz spoke out plain, and said clear what she'd got to say.

She said, a few minutes after mother'd set out for the old Jane's, Nance Darvel came down in the kitchen to make the mistress's gruel. She put it on to warm, and then Nance said, "Let's have a glass of mead, Liz, I fancy 'tis awful chilly?" So she took a bottle out of the cupboard and poured out a glass for Liz, and a glass for herself, and they both of them drank it right off.

Then Nance Darvel took up the mistress's gruel and carried it with her upstairs.

But Liz said that she felt awful sleepy, she couldn't make it out, she thought it must be the mead, but she'd often taken more and never felt so foolish; she tried to put some turfs on the fire, but she nearly fell right down.[14] So she sat herself down in mother's chair, and dropped right off to sleep, and she didn't wake again till she felt Nance Darvel a shaking of her, just fore mother come'd in, and a shouting loud in her ear as the little maid had gone. That was all Liz had to say. That she spake the truth was plain to all who heard, mother believed her, and she saw that the Squire did too.

The Squire sat still for a bit, with his arm on the bar of his chair, and his chin in his hand, thinking deep with a rut scored in his forehead. Then he spake stern and hard.

"Nance Darvel, the nurse, come here!"

She came right up from the bottom of the room, and stood quiet and calm before him; while the master sat looking at her with eyes of steel, like a windhover on the wing, as he'd come to her very soul.[15] And Nance stood there, tall and still, with her black hair showing like jet against her pale face, her thin red lips tight shut, her green eyes half closed, and never blinked an eyelash.

---

14 Turf: a block of peat.

15 Windhover: kestrel.

Sure she was a handsome woman, mother said, though she never could abide her, and there were things already whispered that she didn't like to tell of.

Sudden the Squire sprang up from his chair, gripping tight hold of the arms with his hands, while the veins stood out on them ready to burst.

"Woman!" he cried, "where is my child?"

Nance opened her green eyes wide and slow, and looked straight at the master.

"I do not know," she answered back, and her words dropped as four knocks on a coffin-lid.

And the room was so still, you might have heard a pin drop, but for Granfer Lock's hard breathing, he being subject to asthma, and for sure he'd no business to be there.

"Woman!" the Squire saith again, and mother saw his hand open and shut quick on the arm of his chair. "Woman! where is my child?"

Again Nance answered quiet and slow, "I have told you once and I tell you again, I do not know. I left the room for ten minutes, and when I came back the child was gone, and the mistress could tell me naught, for she was out of her mind."

Mother saw the Squire give a quick gasp, then with one stride fore, he came to where Nance Darvel stood, and looked down upon her.

"Liar, devil, murderess!" he saith between his teeth, "how dare you stand before me and speak that lie."

He caught her by the wrist with such a mighty grip that her wrist-bone snapped like a dry stick, for he was terrible strong, and clear beside himself with trouble, poor gentleman, scarce knowing what he did.

Never, mother saith, in all her life did she ever see anything like Nance Darvel. Her turned a bit white, and staggered like, but she just wrapped her hand round in her white apron, as if she'd scratched her finger, and never once took her green eyes off the master's flashing blue ones. Never once.

"Nance Darvel," the master spoke again, and this time his voice broke terrible, as mother said it wrung her heart-strings to hear him. "Oh woman, woman! Before the devil tempts me to kill you, tell me, tell me for God's sake, where is my little child?"

There weren't a dry eye in the room but Nance Darvel's. She stood there calm and quiet with her eyes on the master's. Once when the master's voice broke, mother see'd her mouth twitch, but that was all. Nance Darvel's eyes didn't seem made for tears. Then she reared up her head a little bit higher.

"If 'twas the last words I have to say," she saith, "I swear to you solemn, I do not know."

Then a terrible thing came to pass. The Squire he raised his hand most surely to strike her down. If ever there was murder in any human creature's eyes, mother saith her see'd it in his. He raised his hand to strike, but it never fell. No, it never fell, for it couldn't.

Nance Darvel the nurse had witched him.

She stood there a minute looking at her evil doing, then she flung back her head and laughed. Then slow, she began walking down the room backward, step by step, slow and sure, with her eyes still on the master's. As she came the folk parted right and left, the women shrinking up against the wall and panting for terror. Step by step she moved down the hall till she came close nigh the door, when she held up her hand and laughed again. (Oh Lord! 'twas a laugh!) Then she looked hard to where the master stood, stiff and straight, as a man turned to stone, and with a quick movement she was out of the door, and had banged it loudly after her.

And the master swayed to and fro, then fell heavy to the ground, and lay still on the oaken floor as one that was dead.

And no person dare leave the room to follow Nance Darvel the *witch*.

CHAPTER III

THE COMING OF THE LITTLE SQUIRE

BUT Nance Darvel she hadn't quite finished her evil doings, though, to see the poor Squire, mother saith, you'd a said she'd done enough, and no mistake. But one bad deed begets another, and that's the truth; and I suppose 'twas that was as it came about.

'Twas through the little Jimmy Sollis, who was cleaning up muck in the yard. Father wouldn't let him into the hall, for he didn't see the use. He was just sure to kick up a worrit, and make a scuffing with his boots, beside it weren't no place for children, so he'd set him to clean up the yard, just to keep him out of the way.[16]

Well, he'd got behind the turf rick, when he saw Nance Darvel come quick down the path, with her apron over her arm. She walked on fast, with her head held high, till she came nigh on the great stone posts of the gates, when who should she meet a-coming through, but the poor, mazed critter, Tom, hugging a white rag tight against his chest, and laughing and chittering to himself. Nance was for passing him, but the white thing caught her eye, and she pulled up sudden and short.

"Give that to me," she saith, pointing to the rag with a kind of ordering way. But the fool he just hugged it all the tighter. Her got straight in front of him and looked right down into his mazed and shifty eyes; and her spake out loud and plain, as if she were telling to a deaf man, so as Jimmy Sollis could hear her clear from where he was behind the turf truck.

---

16 Kick up a worrit: cause worry.

"Drop that rag, you fool!" she saith, "and mind this, that you'll never know where you've found it, so long as you've days to live."

Tom's arms fell to his side, slack and heavy, his jaw dropped, and his eyes seemed fixed, while the white rag fluttered to the ground as a dying bird.

Nance swooped right down, as a windhover after a rabbit, and picked it up quick, then she turned and ran through the gate, and down the lane, as fast as her legs could carry her wicked body.

And that there Jimmy was so terrible scared, that he swore he couldn't have moved hand nor foot, nor if he'd a had fifty mad dogs after him. But he see'd Tom stand where he was for a bit, then stagger up the drive and into the hall, same as if he was drunk.

No person took much account of what the child was telling of at the time, but it came back clearer after mother saith; and her had no doubt but the child spoke the truth, and saw what he said he had.

Lord! you may think how the folks were set telling, there wasn't one as hadn't got something to say of Nance that wasn't like other folks. A pity they hadn't all said so afore, mother saith, instead of telling about it so late.

Her was worrited to death, was mother; what with the Squire lying on a bed of sickness and like to die, and the poor lady's burying, and the gentry coming over from Molton to find out about the child, and her having to put them up, she pretty near went mazed.

But they never found the dear child, and they never tracked nothing to Nance, and though the folks spoke plain to them of what Nance did to the Squire, afore all Withyford parish, they said: " 'twas the lady's death, had been too much for the Squire. And as for the child that was lost, they couldn't track it noway; and if Nance

Darvel were a witch, well, then, she was a damned handsome one." So they mounted their horses, and lifted their hats, and rode back again to Molton.

But handsome or no, they as saw knew better, and Nance found every door locked against her, and no person would take her in. Till then she'd been with the old Miss Fishley, as lived down to the shop, but she with the rest had shut her out, so there was no place to Withyford where she dare lay her head. At last she went to live at the cottage in the Combe, and a rough little place it was, as Shepherd Moon once lived in. Built of rough moor stones and thatched on top with rushes, it made a shelter from the weather, sure you scarce could call it more. 'Twas a terribly lonely place a mile away from the village, right amongst the heath, and close amongst some crooked thorns, that looked pretty enough in summer, but when the winter came looked more like black men's ghosts. 'Twas where the river winds round to the foot of "Witches' Combe."

The folks were glad when she went, though if it had been a mile or two further, they'd have been still better pleased. For since she'd shut her door on Nance, old Miss Fishley to the shop had dwindled right away to nothing, and she knew as Nance had cast the evil eye on her because she wouldn't let her in.

Nance Darvel, she didn't starve out in the Combe, neither. If she didn't care to pay for what she bought, no person dare ask her. She kept her fire in on other folks' turfs, and her crock filled with the Squire's rabbits. For she could snare game, Nance Darvel, as well as other folks, so she weren't likely to starve.

'Twas weeks and weeks afore the Squire got about again, dear soul! and when he did, it was a changed man, and aged away terrible quick. Father he couldn't get him to take no real interest in nought, not in his horses, nor riding, nor nought that he'd done afore. His scarlet coat it hung in the hall, but he never put it on, so mother just carried it away and locked it up in the chest, as it mightn't mind him of things, along with the poor lady's clothes, and the little lost maid's. Those very things that she'd worked night and day to finish.

But those things are better away. And the Grange somehow didn't seem the same place as it was, though mother, she did her best to keep in good fires, and see as the maids did their work.

And father he studied the Squire in every way, trying to get him out about as much as he could.[17] For he didn't hold it as a good thing for a man who had lived in the saddle, and always kept the foxes down, to be mopesing in over the fire with no person but Tom Fool to speak to.[18] But the poor gentleman had lost heart for life, and that's the truth.

But as time went on, weeks and months passing, and mother seeing as 'twas a hopeless thing her trying to rouse him out of his trouble herself, and fearing that if her didn't, something bad might happen, she thought on Squire's sister, who lived up to London, and she got old shoemaker Jones, who was clerk, so a bit of a scholar, to write a letter to the lady, a-telling just how 'twas.

Well, I suppose, he put on the letter just what mother had told him, how that the Squire was so broody since his trouble and took no interest in naught; and she feared if something didn't happen soon to get him out of his ways, he'd just go melancholy and never be himself no more.

Shoemaker Jones he wrote it all out beautiful, and put the lady's name fine on the outside, and I suppose where her lived too, and sent it off by mail next day from Molton. And 'twas after a bit that

---

[17] Studied: considered, cared for.

[18] Mopesing: moping.

the lady's answer came back. She was terrible sorry, she said in the letter, to hear what mother'd got to say concerning the Squire. She'd thought a good deal on what was best to do. But there was only one thing that she thought would be any real cure, and that was, her must part with her boy for a bit. "I know, Thirza," she saith, "as you'll take all care of my boy, the same as if he were your own. I wish I could come myself (her was terrible weakly, poor lady), but I feel that nothing in the world can creep into a tired heart so easily as a little child."

And that was how the young Squire first come'd to Withyford, and sure! 'twas a blessed day that first saw his face inside the Grange doors.

Father he took the gig up so far as Exeter town to fetch him. 'Twas a two days' journey up, and a two days' back. He took plenty of wraps with him, for though 'twas the beginning of June, 'twas sharpish up over night times.

Many and many the times since did mother think on the night that he came. How father carried him into the hall just a sleepy bundle, with only the blessed creature's goldy curls a-running out over. Father'd wrapped him snug, you may depend; he was fast asleep and couldn't have been warmer if safe in his own cot at home. Mother just took the cloaks and all and put him straight into Squire's arms where he sat in front of the fire. And as he lay there, her saith, with the light a-playing over his blessed face and yellow hair, it looked for all the world, her saith, as if the Almighty had sent an angel down from heaven to comfort the master in his trouble, and bring sunshine to the Grange once more.

The master sat there with the child on his knees a-looking at him, and every now and again just softly touching up his curls with his great hand.

Withyford Town, by Gratiana Chanter.

"Mary's boy," he saith to himself, " 'Tis Mary's boy."

"Yes, sir," mother saith, " 'tis the young Squire."

"Ah, to be sure!" he saith, "the young Squire. You want a young one to Withyford, Thirza, for the old one's pretty nigh past his work."

"Never that, sir," saith mother, "for the young Squire can't do without the old one, to show him what his duties be."

"Now, I'll warrant," saith father, "as he'd be a fine one to ride to hounds: and who's to tache un I'd like to know, if it b'aint yourself, Squire, nor show un the way across Forest.[19] No person to Withyford, that certain sure."

Then the blessed mite opened his eyes and laughed right up in the master's face.

"Are you my daddy?" he saith, and put up one bit of a hand and touched the master's white hair soft, as if he couldn't quite make out what it were.

"No, no, my lad. I'm nobody's daddy," the master saith, and his voice broke, and the tears sprang full to his eyes, and mother with father went out of the room quiet, and left him alone with the child.

And so the little master come'd.

'Twas a pretty sight to see they two a-riding out together, for the Squire was a fine man on horseback though lately so bent.

And the little master had the Squire's seat exactly, father said, and sure he was afraid of nought. And everywhere they went, mazed Tom went too, and 'twas certain that the blessed child was doing what he'd come for, though mother could see that the Squire he'd never be the same man as he was afore his great trouble come to him.

---

19 B'aint: ain't.

And sure he felt it a good bit when it came to the little one's going.

But he kept about the place more, and looked into things again more as he used, and would talk about things as must be done against the boy came into the place, and his eyes and thoughts seemed looking forward in a way they hadn't done since the poor lady's death.

CHAPTER IV
THE WITCHING OF TAMSIN BALE

SURE! I can mind myself the next time the little Squire came to Withyford, for I must have been about nine years old, and he just gone ten, and sure! 'twas just at that time that the little maid came to live with Nance Darvel to Witches' Combe, and that Nance she got her name up through Tamsin Bale going mazed.

'Twas said through all Withyford as Nance Darvel could call up dead as well as living, and show them to the folk who asked for them, the same as the "Witch of Endor," and it must have been true from what Liza Ann Fry said, for the maid was a truthful one for all I know, though a flighty one at times.

Well I suppose these maids got telling of courtings and such like, (there was Tamsin Bale, Liza Fry and Nelly Challacombe down to Cross) and how Nance Darvel could tell them their fortunes, and how she could cure, and how she could kill. And they wondered if 'twere truth, sure enough! if Nance could show folks who their husbands were to be, and sure! they'd like to know. Till at last that Liza Fry, who was always a bit daring (and sure she must have had the nerve of a grindstone or her never would have thought of it) saith to the other two,

"Let's go and find out."

"To-night?" saith Tamsin.

"Iss fye, to-night," saith Liz, "what's the good to wait?"[20]

"I'm just right for a moonlight walk," saith Nell, "let's go."

---

[20] Iss fye: lit. 'yes faith'. Used as an assertion or quasi-oath, meaning 'yes, by my faith', 'yes, verily' or 'yes, truly'.

But 'twas a long time before they could get Tamsin Bale to say she'd come along with them, for she was a timid maid and never found it an easy thing to make up her mind to nothing. But Liza Fry, as she most always did, at last her got her way, and they all three started off down the lane that led to Witches' Combe.

'Twas a good mile walk afore they come'd to the moor. 'Twas the end of May, or beginning of June, and the moon was up and the hedges showed white with thorn, while the air was full of the scent of it. They were all three full of spirit and fun, for they were but young maids, with their minds taken up with sweethearts, so the walk down the lane was merry, I reckon! till they came to the edge of the moor.

It stretched dark and soft away from them till it cut the clear light of the sky. All the way up the Combe the stream showed sharp as bits of steel, for the light a-shining on it, and the candle in Nance's window peeped like a red star out of the dimpsey. And the maids stopped still and thought a bit.

There weren't no sound in the Combe but the tinkling of water, falling from step to step as it came tumbling down the Combe, and the whirring of the night-hawk a-wheeling round and round, now far now near, then gone. The wind blew off the moor filled with the cent of March burnings, and the blossom of the thorn trees round about Nance Darvel's cottage. 'Twas a night if ever there was one to fill maids' minds with sweethearts. 'Twas ever since Tamsin Bale had felt the brush of heather under her feet, and see'd the light in Nance's window, that I suppose her began to shake and pant with fear, till at last she saith,

"It b'aint a bit of use telling, Liz Fry, for I can't go a step further."

"Go 'long!" saith Nell, "what's there to be afraid of? Nance's candles b'aint no different to other folks that I know by. Come 'long! you looney! and don't stop telling there."

So both the maids told Tamsin that if she wouldn't come with them her must bide by herself where she was; and they ran off quick leaving Tamsin a-shaking in the heather. But they hadn't got far, bless you!! afore she was after them like a deer, for she couldn't bide by herself so was forced to go on, poor maid. But she kept tight hold of Liza's arm the whole way, and when at last they knocked at Nance's door, she screamed right out.

They heard Nance inside a-whispering, then a door open and shut, and something heavy, maybe a table, pushed out of the way; then at last Nance calling through the door, "who be you? and what do'ee want?"

I don't suppose as any of them was feeling quite so brave as when they started, but Liz answered quick and loud,

"Three maidens Nance; as wants to find their husbands."

They heard her laugh behind the door, and then she drew back a bolt and opened it. "Come in my dears," she saith, "and sure you shall see your husbands."

So they all three went in, poor Tamsin clutching on all the whiles tight to Liza Ann's arm.

'Twas a small place where they were, with he floor made of stones taken rough from the earth as they were, and full of pits and cracks. There weren't much in the room by way of furniture. A rough table, a couple of benches, a great chest in the corner, with the settle round the fire, was I reckon, about all of it. There was a turf fire, a-blazing on the hearth, a black crock bubbling and singing over it, and bunches and bunches of dried herbs a-hanging from the rafters.

All three maidens sat down on the settle, and Nance, she just swept up the hearth with an old besom, put two or three turfs on the fire, then turned again, and asked them what they wanted.[21]

Liz saith, her felt all the daring go right out of her, soon as Nance looked hard at her with wicked green eyes. But her made up her mind her'd go through with it, whatever happened. For she weren't no coward was Liza Ann Fry, whatever else her was.

A-squatting in the midst of the floor, staring and a-swallowing was a bloated toad most terrible to look at, poor Tamsin, she couldn't take her eyes off it.

"Whatever do ye keep that awful reptile there for Nance?" Liz saith. "I shouldn't rest until I'd killed it dead, and heaved it out on the dung-heap."

"That's my business, Liz Fry," saith Nance, "and not yours. He's a dear friend of mine," she saith with a laugh, "and worth all the Withyford folk a-put together."

"A dear friend, indeed!" saith Liz as peart as she could.[22] "Well, if he was one of that sort, I'd rather be without him for my part," but she daren't say much, or she feared as Nance wouldn't tell her what she'd come for.

"So 'tis sweethearts you're hunting," saith Nance, laughing again. "I should have thought as three pretty mids as you be, weren't wanting for one apiece, and some to spare."

"Us b'aint neither," saith Nell, with a toss of her head. "It ain't sweethearts we'm wanting you to show us. Nance Darvel, 'tis husbands. They'm different."

"You're right my dear," saith Nance with a sneer, "you're right they'm different; well, bide just where you be, and before you get

[21] Besom: a broom made from thin twigs.

[22] Peart: cheerful, lively.

up from that there settle, I swear you shall see them; now listen to what I tell ye."

"You must bide as quiet as mice when the cat's after them, while I dout the fire and the candle, and then just you look before you, against the wall."

She went over to the table, and blew the candle out, but the fire was so bright, it didn't make much difference, so she threw some water on, as filled the room with smitch, but still left the turfs with a goodish glow in them, as they could see Nance Darvel's tall shape moving about quite plain.[23]

She stood in the middle of the room with a long stick in her hand; and on the floor at her feet, just where the glow of the fire struck, sat that filthy toad, a-swallowing and a-swallowing.

"Now!" saith Nance, in a slow soft way, (different to how she'd been speaking), "now Liz, look at your husband." Her made three or four strokes against the wall with her long stick thing, and sure a feint yellow light began to show all over the part where she'd drawn, and stayed there on the wall. *Then*, (and this be the truth, Liz saith, if 'twas the last words she ever spoke), out of that light, the face of a man began to shape itself. It came a bit slow at first, showing out in the misty light, and then going back again. Then sudden for two minutes or such, she saw it quite plain, and so did Nell Challacombe; and if ever they'd see'd Bill Fishley's face afore, it was hanged up then on Nance Darvel's wall, as real as ever they'd seen it in life.

The maidens they screamed outright and Liz she was in a proper way too, for 'twasn't Bill she want at all, but Jack Curtis up to Molesworthy. Then Nance she made another stroke with her

---

[23] Smitch: smoke.

stick and the light went out on the wall, and the room was dimpsey as before. Liz could feel Tamsin a-shuddering and a-shaking by her side, and could see her eyes by the firelight, almost starting out of her head. Then Nance saith slow and deeplike,

"Now Nell Challacombe!"

When the light came again on the wall, slow and sure Johnny Light the pedlar come'd along with it. As clear as day they all three saw him, staring at them with his cross eyes as natural as life.

"Lord! Nance Darvel," screamed Nell, a-jumping up, I'm never going to have he? Why! he's cross-eyed and pummel-footed, and b'aint exactly there," and I suppose her was in a proper way about it and fell to crying.[24]

And by that time, I reckon! they were all wishing pretty strong that they hadn't come nigh the cursed place at all. Then Nance saith,

"I can only show you the truth; you asked for it and you've got it. Look, Tamsin Bale!"

Liz always believes that if Tamsin she'd had the breath, she'd have called out and told Nance to stop 'fore she got any further. But she was so properly choking for fear that her couldn't speak one word.

The light came again, just as the other two had done, but Lord! what came in the midst of it the third time neither Liz nor Nell, *dare* nor *could* say. For 'twas something so terrible ugly, so hellish and evil, that that there witch Nance Darvel herself stood a gasping at what she'd dragged up, for 'twas a more awful sight you may depend than mortal man could dream of or mortal tongue could tell.

Liz and Nell looked once then hid their faces quick, and shook as if they'd got the ague. But Tamsin her sat there as if turned

---

[24] Pummel-footed: club-footed or clumsy.

to stone, then sudden she flinged up her hands, and threw herself down on the floor, and screamed, and screamed, and screamed. And there the awful thing stayed like a bit out of hell on the wall of the witch's place.

"Put it out! put it out! for God's sake Nance," cried Liz, "do ye wish to drive all three of us raving mazed afore the night's out?"

Nance came up close to Liz and breathed hard in her ear.

"I can't," she sort of hissed, "I can't, for I've forgotten *how*, stop that girl screaming, Liz, stop her! Why don't she stop?"

Poor Tamsin she lay there on the stones, a-screaming and writhing awful, and that beastly toad hopped slowly round her head a-swallowing.

And still, though they dare not look again, they knew the awful thing was there.

Nance came over and kneeled down by the maid, then put her fingers tight on Tamsin's head, and looked hard at her for a minute or two. And Tamsin she gave just one big sort of sob, and stopped short in midst of an awful screech, and lay on the ground quite still.

And Nance, her got up with her stick and they suppose she *remembered*, for when they looked up again the fearsome thing had left them.

And how they got back that night they scarce could tell. For Tamsin Bale, poor soul, was mazed till the day her died, and 'twas a mercy when her went. That the poor maid had been witched out of her wits by Nance Darvel every person to Withyford knew, and Nance you may depend, was more feared and hated than before.

And 'twas fact that they maidens were married to Johnny Light and Bill Fishley, though 'twas many years after. For the maidens they gave them the hoist more than ever, through Nance having picked them out for them, and the memories of that awful night in the Combe was dead against their courtings. But however in time it came to pass just as Nance Darvel had said.

Though you may depend ’twas many a year ’fore they went to the Combe again.

CHAPTER V

THE HUNTING OF THE MAY HARE

IT was Abr'am Ash who was out over turf cutting, as first telled of seeing the little maid to Witches' Combe. He was up on top and came home and telled as how he'd swear as sure as he was a living man, there was a child biding out long with Nance Darvel to Witches' Combe. For he'd watched her playing about a good half hour, till Nance had a-come out and called her in.

Folks didn't take much account of it, knowing as Abr'am knew how to tell lies, and thinking 'twas one of his. Folks had been saying all sorts, since the witching of Tamsin Bale, and one scarce knew what to believe and what not to. But all telled it for certain truth, and 'twas no longer a matter for doubting, when father came home and told of the running of the May hare, and of the wonderful doings of the little Squire.

Father'd been out over exercising the puppies, with the little Squire and mazed Tom to keep them all together. They was coming down over Lawney Cleve on the ways home, and father he was telling to the little Squire, and so not taking much account of the dogs, when sudden Vagrant he started a hare, and afore father could so much as smack his whip, they was all a streaming down the valley in full cry, looking beautiful I'll warrant, for I've see'd them many's the times in the brown heath, running even, and showing white as pearls along a string.

And sure, father said there was nought to do but to follow them on as hard as they could, and whip them off so soon as they got the chance. Though he was in a fine way, and fell out with mazed Tom, for not looking sharper after them, nor to see what they were doing.

But the little Squire, he was just pleased, you may believe! cracking of his whip and hollowing as lusty as father hiself, and keeping as near the hounds as he could.

Well, I suppose they rode like this here for a good mile or more, the hare going wonderful straight and the hounds running pretty. The Combe began getting a bit rough with boulders, stones and such like, being bad going for the horses and giving the hounds a chance of getting ahead. Sudden they turned where a spur of yellow fuzz showed in the brown of the heath, and one by one like beads on a string they slipped round the curve out of sight.[25]

It weren't more than three seconds, father said, afore they was on them again, and there they were all leaping and jumping round a little maid standing under a rock, fighting them off with a yellow fuzz bush in her hand, while the valley rang and rang with their noise as if all the bells to Withyford had been set a-pealing.

He gave one look, father saith, and then he digged his spurs into the mare's sides and rode, as he'd only once done afore in his life.

But hard as he rode, the little Squire he kept up with him, and quick as he was, the little Squire he was quicker.

Like a flash he was in the middle of the hounds, a-laying about him like a man with no thought of fear in his head.

Right and left, and left and right he sent the dogs a-howling. Sure 'twas a brave sight to see him, for afore father could get nigh, he'd both his arms, dear lad, about the little maid, kissing of her and telling her not to mind, for sure he was there to look after her, and while he was by she'd come to no harm.

As soon as father'd a-got the hounds well in, he turned his mind upon the little maid where her stood against the rock with

25 Fuzz: furze, gorse.

the little Squire a-coaxing of her. He said sudden it come'd upon him like a flash, and it properly took his breath away to think upon it.

He knew every child to Withyford, did father, for he was terrible fond of children, and they of he, always calling after him when they saw his scarlet coat. But this was no Withyford maid, and there was only one thing he could think of, and he didn't like the looks of it.

No, you may depend he didn't, for this was how he thought it out.

The hare they was running had gone! where? and there in its place stood a strange child, and that child no other than a witch's child. Many and many's the times he'd heard as witches and hares was one and the same, and now he'd seen it for hiself. And he scarce knew what to think nor do, for it properly made him cream all over to see the little Squire a-touching of her, thinking of all that had gone afore.[26]

"Let her alone Squire," father saith sharp, "taint for such as you to be kissing of a witch's maid. Lord knows what she might do to ye. Let her alone I say! harm enough has come through them to you and yours, and the farther off you keep from her the better."

But the young Squire he laughed right out and kissed the little maid again, just for a bit of daring. And nought would satisfy him but she must ride behind him on the cob, so far as Shallyford, where the track leads away from the hollow up over to Witches' Combe.

"Who are you, little maid?" he saith, as she sat tight up behind him, a-gripping of his belt.

"Who are you, and where do you come from?"

---

[26] Cream: go pale.

"I be Malvina," she saith, "and I live to Combe, up over, long with Nance Darvel."

Then Father he knew it for certain.

They set her down to Shallyford, and sure, father saith, as she stood there among the rushes, she looked a proper picture, and no mistake, with her soft curls blowing and a-lifting with the breeze, and her lovely face a-showing from her dark frock, like a lily from its leaves, and the bunch of yellow fuzz still clasped in her hands.

"Good-bye Malvina, and don't you go and cry," saith the little Squire.

Then he took the silk handkerchief from his neck to wipe her eyes with, and told her she might have it for a keep-sake.

"Just one more kiss," he saith, and afore father could stop him, he'd kissed her again where she stood, with the tears a-trembling on her eyelids, and the yellow bunch in one hand, and the red kerchief in the other.

"When fuzz be out of blossom, kissing be out of fashion," he shouted, as he jumped on the cob, and rode away down Combe, waving his hand to the little maid where she stood amongst the rushes.

You may depend as father and mother watched him sharp for many days after that, fearing what might be the outcome of that day. And in particular as the little Squire was aways telling of Malvina, and wanting to go to the Witches' Combe to see her. But father he managed clever to keep him t'other side of Withyford, and afore the time came for him to go back again to London, they fancied he'd forgotten most nigh all about it.

CHAPTER VI

MALVINA, THE WITCH'S MAID

AS years went on, things kept much the same to Withyford. Granfer Lock he was dead, and so was the old Jane Bowden, poor Tamsin Bale going afore them both.

The young Squire he came down from time to time, but only for a few days together, and that a long way between, for being took up with his education. But old Squire was always mighty pleased to see him, and so for the matter of that, were all the folks of Withyford. For as he was as boy, so he was as man, like the sunshine coming into a cold place.

The old Squire he just grew older and more bent, and the stricken look that was in them never quite left his eyes. But he kept about, and no person dare gainsay him, no more than afore his trouble came upon him. Nance Darvel she didn't let the folks forget her neither, what with witching thirty of Farmer Jan's sheep, so as every one of them died in one night, and a-marking Mal Lock's face with a red scar from ear to chin, which she carried to her grave, folks weren't likely to forget. Though she'd been quiet for the last year, sure! quieter than folks had ever known her.

'Twas rare now that she walked down Withyford street, and they who saw, said that she looked terrible changed, and mortal bad in the face. They'd think she was suffering for all her wicked doings, and it served her right.

But most times now at shop or on any other errand, she sent the maid Malvina, though the poor child was almost as much hated as Nance herself, and no person ever poke of her except as "Malvina, the Witch's Maid."

It weren't right you may depend for folks to be so hard on the maid as they were, for no persons knew ought against her excepting her lived with Nance. She was just a beauty to look to, and maybe the women folk were a bit harder for that same reason.

There were two or three boys that were after her, and would have given much I'll warrant for a look or a kiss. but she never took no notice of any, passing them by with her head held high and her eyes looking straight afore her.

The young Jan Williams up to Bartin was one, 'twas supposed to be a settled thing between him and Joan Richards, but Bill Crocombe (who was at the time courting me) saith he knew for certain sure, as there was only one in the world for Jan, and that one was Malvina. But it was no use Jan Williams a-setting his mind that way for his father would see him dead before he'd let him have her.

And Malvina her'd have nothing to say to Jan certain sure. She knew very well as he wouldn't be seen with her in daylight, and her was too proud a maid by a long way, to put up with his sneaking round after her in the dark. Many and many's the times he waited for her going out to the Combe, by the first gate in the lane, and was properly mad with her because she'd have nothing to say to him.

"Let me carry your basket, Malvina my dear," he'd say, "sure 'tis too heavy for that pretty arm of your'n. You'd best let me carry it for you, do'ee now."

"I can carry my basket myself, Jan William," she'd make answer, "they as won't help me in the light, shan't help me in the dark, and that you'll understand." And then her'd walk on with her head held high, and her eyes looking straight afore her, while Jan walked alongside. "Malvina," he'd say, "now don't you be in such a way, 'tis father I'm afeared on, not the folks. If it came to his ears as I was walking out with you he'd near kill me, and as for Joan her'd——"

"It's nought to me what Joan or your father do," her'd say quick and proud, "you and your's are nothing to me and I don't want to hear ought about them. But I do know this, and I've told 'ee afore, that the less you come to the Combe Lane in the dimpsey the better I'll be pleased, and the sooner you moves out of it to-night the sooner I'll thank you," and her'd speak haughty, and her eyes would give little flashes.

But these here ways of her's, bless you! only made Jan Williams all the more mazed about her, for he was used to having his own mind with most of the maids to Withyford.

He was a bit of a catch, and a handsome boy and well set up, so the maidens they didn't turn their backs on him you may be sure. 'Twas Malvina's ways being so different, I reckon, as made him think all the more on her.

And of course 'twas just at this time that mother got Malvina working up to Grange.

Mother she went out to shop one day. She'd run short of dips, and her wanted to see the old Miss Fishley too, as she was fast going home, the old woman had done nought for some time back, and since Liz had married, she'd looked after the shop.[27]

Mother got her dips and telled with Liz a bit, and then her went up and sat with old Miss Fishley; but she didn't stop long, her was so weakly poor soul, and mother she feel'd it a good bit, thinking maybe 'twas the last time she'd see her, for she'd known Miss Fishley all her days, and she took anything like that to heart, did mother, for her was always terrible feeling hearted.

---

[27] Dips: dip-candles.

Well she'd got a little way down the street when her heard a shouting and a calling out, and there standing under the lilac bushes with her back against the wall by Bill Smith's was Malvina.

There was a dozen or so children round her led by that there Jimmy Vellacott, yelling and screeching at the tops of their voices, and a throwing of muck and pixy's stools at her, and calling out that her was a witch.[28]

There was one boy, he took up a stone and threw it so that it struck her and the blood ran. The poor maid turned dreadful white and dropped her basket, and if mother hadn't come up at that very minute, she believed as the children would have had everything as was in it. But they were so taken up with a-worriting the maid that they never saw mother till she was close nigh on them, and just as that little varmint was ready to fling another stone, she caught him such a clout right under the ear as sent him flying into the whole lot, startling them pretty fine I'll warrant.

As soon as they saw it was mother it didn't take them long to get round the corner and out of sight, for though mother were so feeling hearted, her was hottish with her tongue when she was set up.

Malvina, poor maid, stood leaning against the old wall just faint with the blow, and feeling as if she couldn't move so much as to pick up the things as was scat in the road.[29]

Mother never could tell how it come about, but it seemed no time afore she'd filled Malvina's basket for her and had got her into Grange kitchen, a-bathing of her head, while she sat in father's chair, listening to all her'd got to say, though that wasn't much.

---

[28] Pixy's stools: toadstools, mushrooms.

[29] Scat: scattered.

For the maid was shy and proud, and if she hadn't been real bad, mother didn't believe that she'd ever have got her inside Grange doors. But there was something about the maid that took mother wonderful. 'Tweren't altogether her beautiful face (though that ought to have been enough for most folks) but mother'd a feeling as soon as she saw her standing there, with those wicked children round her, that witch or no witch, her must do all in her power to help her.

I don't think as I ever saw father more put out with mother, than when she told him what her'd done, and that if Nance Darvel'd let her, her was going to have the maid up once a fortnight to help in the kitchen; for her thought as folks were treating the maid shameful, and her for one wouldn't stand by and see it done.

"I should think, Thirza, as you'd seen enough of witching to last ye," father saith with a sneer, "without encouraging one of those kind about the place. I thought you'd more sense, why I *know* the maid be a witch, I've told 'ee so, scores of times, since I saw with my own eyes what happened out to Shallyford."

"Get along with your nonsense!" saith mother, with a toss of her head, though I saw she half believed him, and was wondering to herself if she hadn't let her warm heart outstep her reason. 'Twas a way she had, and she knew it.

" 'Taint no nonsense," saith father, "and that you'll find out I reckon, when one of us be witched into our graves."

"Us must all go there sometime," saith mother, "that's certain, and 'tis no odds as I can see if us be dropped in, or witched in. 'Twon't turn *my* hair grey a thinking on it."

Father he just went out of the kitchen, for he weren't a good one to argue, and mother she looked red and give'd the cat a clout as sent her flying.

But Malvina she came regular to Grange once in every two weeks, and took to mother wonderful and mother to her.

But father he watched her about, and wouldn't never go nigh her though the maid was wonderful pretty in her ways. And Malvina was quick to see that he didn't like her, and held her head high and looked straight and proud, whenever he was about, while to mother he was ever suent.[30]

[30] Suent: pleasant, agreeable, kindly.

CHAPTER VII
THE CROSSHAND DANCE

IT was a sharp Christmas that year, I mind. There was a heavy snowfall on the Friday and then the frost set in, and the roads was all to one glidder making it properly difficult to get about.[31]

The river was frozen over down to Ford, a thing the oldest liver scarce could mind, and as rarely happened, by reason of the quick running of the water.

The young folks liked the cold, making slipper-slides, and having games with the snow, and finding it an easy job to track the rabbits and birds. But it was a bad job for the dumb creatures and they as looked after the sheep, and those who were old and whose blood crept slow in their veins; sure for them it was terrible bad!

To be sure, I mind that Christmas well; and many's the times when sitting quiet here, I look a long ways back and think deep on the hows and whys of things. For Bill Crocombe and me was courting then.

We used to walk together in the lane at the bottom of Grange Gates, and sure 'twas mortal cold. But sweethearts be sweethearts all the world over, and weather, and wind, and rain, don't make much difference to them, so long as they've got each other.

'Twas so with Bill and me. I'd just put mother's old widdle over my head and then out to meet him down by the Linhay so soon as I heard his whistle.[32] For there was often more company in the Grange kitchen than they who were courting cared much

---

31 Glidder: frosted, slippery.

32 Widdle: a cape or shawl.

about, and sweethearts have things to say, and ways as they don't want the whole world to know.

I can mind every bit of the road as if those walks were taken but yesterday. How the trees were all to one sparkle and glitter, and the moors rolling off and away in great drifts beyond the sooty oakwoods in the hollow. The stars above were just as bright as the frost below, and all was wonderful still. And how our breath went up like steam from a kettle, and the smell of frost in the air.

There were forty red-deer as came down every night to the cleve across the Combe. Bless you! they wouldn't have come so nigh to Withyford if it hadn't been mighty cold out over and the fodder uncommon scarce.

'Twas on Christmas Eve, and just such a night as I've been telling of, as all Withyford was met together in the great hall up to the Grange, for dancing, supper, and such like. The young master he was down, and nought would please the old one, but as all the folks should come up there to make merry, and enjoy themselves, by way of keeping Christmas.

'Twas mostly left to mother, but her was a clever one to manage, I can tell you, and sure, the supper looked splendid, laid out on tables the whole length of the kitchen.

'Twas about seven when they started the dancing. They put Jimmy Crick on the table in the window, and there he sat with a jug of ale beside him (for they do say as fiddling be terrible thirsty work), and there he sat a-tuning up, and screwing of his fiddle, and telling to Johnny Light, as to what dance they'd have. For Johnny Light, though crippled and pummel-footed too, was a proper man to set the dancing going, though the one to dance off all the lot was Billy Coats the chimney-sweep, my! he could go!

The old Squire was up at the higher end of the hall, close against the fire, and the young Squire stood beside him. They were telling with some of the old folk, Farmer Jan, and Farmer Will, amongst the number. The old Squire's hair showed white against the black oak of his chair, and his eyes, for all the world like a hawk's, were shining brighter than I'd seen them for many a year.

Ah Lord! poor soul! 'twas no wonder they'd grown dim!

And the young Squire, bless him! why, you could hear him laugh from one end of the hall to the other, it did one good to hear him. And sure, he was a beautiful man to look at, as he stood there on the hearth with his golden curls a-shining in the light, same as the time when mother carried him into that very hall, nigh fifteen years agone, though now he was six feet two, and as broad across the shoulders as Dick the blacksmith.

'Twas a pretty sight that Christmas party up to Grange. For 'tis always pretty and full of life, where men and maidens meet with a wish to enjoy themselves, and the old folk by, to see there b'aint too much foolishness.

The men and maidens were all forming up for a crosshand dance, and showing out plainly against the dark oak walls. They took some time making up their minds as to what partners they would choose, and Joan Richards for one had refused three or four, as thinking Jan Williams would ask her. But Jan was another way about.

Mother was in the kitchen, just patching up a goose with a bit of parsley (as the cat had taken a bit out of it, through the door being left open), when Jan Williams he put his head in and saith quick and eager like,

"Where be Malvina hiding to?"

"What do'ee want to know that for?" mother answered sharp, "her don't want ye courting her in the dark, when you won't speak to her in the light like a man. I'd be ashamed to behave like that there to so fine a maid, if I was you, Jan Williams," mother saith.

Jan Williams he looked at mother straight, and shut his lips tight. He was a fine black-eyed, black-haired boy was Jan, and well set up. He had a look on his face that night, mother saith, as if he'd made up his mind to do something, and do it he would, and 'twould be a strong man as would turn him from his purpose. She noticed too that he was pale in the face for him, and slighter than he used to be. "Sure he's in earnest about Malvina," her thought to herself.

"Tell me where the maiden be," saith Jan, "and then I'll promise you Thirza, that both you and Withyford shall see afore long, why for I want her."

"Lord!" saith mother, with a sneering laugh, as if her didn't believe him, "then that will be something new I warrant. Well, she's out in the passage there; but she won't thank me for the telling."

Malvina was up at the higher end of the passage, peeping through the little window that looks into the hall. She was standing on tiptoe watching the folk inside. The passage was long and dimpsey, except right under the window, and she was so taken up with what was going on that she never knew as Jan Williams was nigh till he was right close upon her, and sure, then her jumped with fear.

"Don't ye be a-feard," he saith, " 'tis only me. Thirza, she said you was here; I was wanting you and asked. Though she reckoned," he saith bitterly, "as you'd soon have my room as my company."

Malvina she turned round, and lent with her back against the wall under the window, so as the light fell on her lovely curls, and her face was in the shadow, but not so much as Jan couldn't see every bit of its beauty, nor the haughty look in her great eyes, as she looked straight at him.

"What do you want me for?" she said.

"To dance," he saith.

Malvina lifted her brows and looked prouder than before.

"With who?" she asked.

"With me," saith Jan.

Malvina keped her wonderful eyes on him while he stood there, poor lad, with his face white and working; for he was as strong in love with her as a man can be, and her coolness near drove him mazed.

Malvina held up her hand, and marked off each word with her finger.

"*You* want me to dance with *you*," her saith; "*you*, Jan Williams, afore the whole of Withyford parish, to dance with *me*, 'Malvina, the Witch's Maid!' Do you know what you're telling? Jan Williams."

And she threw back her head and laughed, a little bitter sneering laugh, as showed her pearls of teeth, and the whiteness of her throat, but weren't a happy thing to hear from the mouth of a maid.

"Malvina, you don't believe me," he cried! " 'fore God I mean it!"

And then, I suppose, she saw he did, for her cheeks flushed up and her eyes flashed, and her saith, slow and thoughtful-like,

"Jan Williams, you be a brave man, and I like you for it. I most surely do."

"*Like* me," he cried with his eyes upon her, "Oh Malvina, sweetheart, why I love you, I love you, and there's nought upon this earth that I wouldn't do for you! Listen and hark to what I'm telling, Malvina!"

Just to that moment Jimmy Crick he struck up with his fiddle, and the folks started inside with the crosshand dance. Jan had hold of both Malvina's hands, and in another moment he'd have had his lips on her's, but with a quick twist she loosened herself from him, and down the passage she flew like a bird, and where the full light streamed in from the hall door, she waited a moment for him, with her finger on her lips.

"Now," she whispered soft, while her eyes shone and her breath came quick, "Now Jan, be you ready to take the consequence?"

He just looked down at her and took her hand tightly within his, and led her right into the hall.

They'd begun the crosshand dance at the bottom of the room. Johnny Light, he was capering about fine. 'Twas strange how active he was to be sure considering how whirlfooted he was.[33] Jan he led Malvina through the room thinking to get her into the dance quiet without no notice being taken; but that weren't to be.

No person could see such a couple as those two, a-coming along hand in hand, without taking two looks at them. Malvina had on her dark stuff dress, with a red handkerchief about her neck, and a bunch of holly at her breast, and as her walked up the room with her head held high, and her eyes a-shining like two stars, she looked like a queen for sure, and so thought more than one.

Mother was standing close behind the two Squires when Malvina she first came in sight. She saw the old man start and catch hold to the arms of his chair, while the young master just took a step back, and saith quick in her ear,

"Who the devil is that girl, Thirza? What a beauty! Where on earth have you hidden her? Why she steps like a queen! Jove! what a beauty!"

"Her be Malvina;" mother saith quiet, "and her lives out to Witches' Combe."

---

[33] Whirlfooted: club-footed.

"Good Lord!" he saith, "and I've seen many a duchess who'd have given every diamond she possessed to walk through a room like that. What a perfect head? Thirza woman, I can't make it out."

And he never took his eyes off her from that moment, no more did the old Squire.

As ill luck would have it, Jan got Malvina into the crosshand dance just alongside of Joan Richards. He see'd a bit of a gap and took her right in never noticing who was next to him, though he'd have given his eyes to have changed it the moment he saw how it was.

Malvina in passing touched Joan's arm, and Joan she turned in a moment and saw who was next. Her face grew crimson with rage, and her flinged right out of the dance altogether.

"I b'aint going to stand next to Witch's Maid!" her said, tossing her head, "not very likely!"

She spoke out shrill and clear so as all the room heard her, and the folks stopped dancing, and Jimmy Crick a-fiddling. "How dare such a one come along with *us*?" screamed Joan, stamping her foot. She was fairly beside herself with rage, seeing who 'twas had brought Malvina into the dance, and she didn't care what she said. For Joan had a terrible tongue, and knew how to use it, and when she was in one of her rages, no person could stop her.

The folk had all drawn away from Malvina, and every eye in the room was on the maid. Maybe there was a man or two among them who would have liked to have said a word for her, only Joan's tongue was too much for them. As for the women folk, well some was really feared of her, and the rest thought it best to leave her alone, and were curious to see what would happen.

Jan he came over and took Malvina's hand, and then Joan went properly mad.

"You daring witch!" she saith, "a-coming along of respectable folk. Who knows what they may wake up with to-morrow, spotted faces and all sorts? Ah! you wicked, daring thing; go back to Witches' Combe and bide there, for you won't find as decent folk will have anything to do with ye. Look to Jan Williams there!" she cried with a shrill laugh, pointing with her finger, while her face just flamed with passion, "witched, if ever a man was witched, so as he can't help following her wherever she goes whether he likes it or no. You'd best look out," her saith with a sneering laugh to the other maids, " 'twill be your turn soon, and not a maid to Withyford will be able to keep her man."

Malvina took her hand from Jan's and moved a step away from him, and seeing she wished it, so he let her be, though his heart was just yearning to fight them all for her sake.

So the maid stood by herself, quiet and tall, holding her head like a queen's, while a red spot burned on either cheek, and she caught her lip tight between her snowy teeth.

When Joan had fairly given in because she'd no more breath; Malvina her just looked round to all the folk as if she'd strip their very souls; and more than one shrank back from her as her clear eye flashed. And then she spoke, and every word her saith came out as clear as a bell.

"You need not be afeared, any of you," her saith; "for I be going. But afore I do go, I ask you plain all in this here room, have I ever done ought to harm any man, woman, or child to Withyford Town? They lie who say I have, and you know it! You be cowards all, and I scorn you as the dirt under my feet. Touch you?" she cried, while her sweet lips trembled, "dance with you? mix with you? no, never again, you need not be afeard, I be going!"

And she turned quickly round, her eyes bright with anger,

her lips all to a quiver, and walked swiftly down the room towards the door.

But afore she got there, the young Squire was alongside of her.

"Please stay one moment," he saith, "for I want you to dance with me, that is to say if you will, Malvina; strike up Jimmy!" And afore Malvina knew where she was, her was up the middle and down again, with the young Squire's arm about her waist, and his strong young hand in hers. And you may be sure as there wasn't one in the room as dare question the young Squire's partner.

The moment as Jimmy Crick had stopped the dance through giving in with his fiddle, Malvina, she slipped from the Squire's arms, afore he knew, and was out of the door, and into the kitchen to mother. Her breath was coming quick, mother saith, and her eyes shone like two stars, and her cheeks were glowing as roses fresh picked.

"I must be going," her saith. "Goodbye Thirza!" and she unhung her cloak from the door and began a-putting of it on.

"You surely b'aint going yet awhile?" mother saith, "why, the folks haven't had supper yet, and how can I get along with only Liz? I can't get on without ye, my dear!"

"But you *must*, Thirza," her saith quick and sharp. "Now don't go and stop me, there's a dear soul! I b'aint going to face one of they folk again to-night, no, never again if I can help it. For I've been shamed afore the whole of Withyford, and I'm going to give no person the chance of doing it again. I was foolish even to put foot inside these doors, to-night be the last time I've a-done it."

Malvina's hands were trembling, so as she scarce could tie up her hood. The tears were standing on her lashes, but her face kept proud and haughty for all that. Mother saw as it weren't a bit of use to try and turn her from her purpose, so she just let her be, and said nought. But she felt a bit sore to think as Malvina should speak so, for 'twas only for the maiden's good that she'd brought her at all to Grange.

Sudden, as if Malvina guessed what mother was thinking, she kissed her quick and got her lovely arms about her.

"Now don't you, don't you, Thirza," her saith, "go and think ought against me. You be the only person in the world who cares a scat about me, and that I know.[34] I b'aint ungrateful, and you mustn't think it, but I can't come to Grange again. I can't, I *can't*!"

"There, there,"saith mother, "don't take on so, dear maid. There be other folk a love ye, without old Thirza. Oh yes there be, and time will make mention who?"

"Hush!" Malvina said, "there be someone coming!" and afore mother could stop her, she was out of the door and round the back, and in another minute she heard her quick feet pass the window, and the crisp frost crackling under her tread.

---

[34] Scat: fig.

CHAPTER VIII

HOW MALVINA QUESTIONED NANCE

AS Malvina neared the cottage, her heart beat quick and fast, for she was making up her mind to do that which she'd never dared do afore. Things had come to such a pass that night as set her wondering, her mind was filled with thoughts as wouldn't keep silent, and her whole being rebelled near past controlling.

She lifted the latch of Nance's door, but 'twas locked, so she gived a rap with her knuckles.

She heard the push of a chair across the floor and the slip of Nance's feet coming to her, then a wooden bar was lifted, and Nance let her in. Malvina went to the fire and knelt down; Nance, her stood with the candle in her hand, looking at her.

Nance had altered terrible, I suppose, and bent wonderful, and looked as one who was always in racking pain, and cursed the Almighty for giving it to them. And I recon as that was true, though she'd only her own wickedness to thank for it. Her face was that sallow and properly lined with wrinkles, her grisly locks hung loose about her face, while her eyes burned like green fires in her head, and her looked like one, as she stood there, as death had marked for his own.

Malvina, she knelt in front of the fire a-warming her hands, but she'd said no word to Nance since her'd come in, nor Nance to her.

She was to have stayed over Christmas day to Grange, and she knew as Nance was wondering what had brought her back, and both were waiting for the other to speak first.

"Well Grannie," her saith at last, without looking up, "you be wondering, b'aint you, what's brought me back. If you'll sit down I'll tell you," and her went on warming her hands.

Nance muttered to herself and looked as if her'd like to say more; but she put her candle down, and hobbled to her corner in the settle close against the fire, and sat with her green eyes on Malvira waiting for her to speak.

Then Malvina sprang to her feet, and told her quick and fast all as had happened to the dance at the Grange, and how Joan Williams had called her "witch" afore them all.

And Nance watched her all the while as the maid moved back and fore with the feelings as came over her, through going through the troubles that had happened, and when she came to the part where the young Squire had come up and taken her hand afore them all, the lights shot green from Nance's eyes, and she rubbed her hands together.

"Then! then!" Malvina saith, "I left them all forever, for nevermore will I put my foot inside Grange doors, nor go where folks call me 'witch.' "

Nance laughed shrill and high from her corner and rubbed her hands again.

"No, no, my lady," her chuckled, "they shall fetch thee when they want thee, sure enough, yes fye; from Witches' Combe."

Malvina had worked herself up, her cheeks were flaming and her two eyes glowing like stars, she'd got more to say to Nance afore she'd done, and her was just ready to say it.

"I made up my mind coming homewards, Grannie," she went on, "as I'd ask you plain what this here means. Why be the folks always telling of witches and witching? Why be I hounded and shrunk from as if I was some evil being; I, who have never done harm to any living creature? Why do they call me 'Malvina, the Witch's Maid,' and no other name at all? Why be I hated and cursed and pointed at? Why, oh why, I ask ye?"

She came forward to the full light of the fire, and stood in front of Nance, half begging her, half defying. She was putting all her strength into what she said, for she felt it must be to-night or never.

"I've asked ye again and again, Grannie, and you've always put me off, but to-night it shall not be," her saith, "no it shall not be, you shall tell me all I ask, or I leave this place to-morrow and never set foot in it again."

Her voice was clear and firm with no touch of a tremble in it, Nance moved a bit and dropped her lids half over her eyes, a trick her had when her was extra watchful and plotting something deep.

"You shall tell me first of all," saith Malvina, "who and what I be, do you hear Grannie? who and what I be?"

"A lady, a lady, my dear," Nance croaked, and she rocked herself back and fore as she said it, with an evil look in her eyes, "You'm a lady, lady to be sure!"

" 'Tis always the same old nonsense," Malvina cried, "oh Grannie, I'm tired to death of it. A lady indeed," she saith, and she swinged herself round with a bitter laugh, for her was full of trouble, poor maid.

"Now listen," her saith, and turned to Nance once more. "I've gone through that to-night as had made me bitter and hard, I know you be terrible ill, and 'tis cruel to leave you alone, sure, but I go from this place to-morrow unless you tell me. Naught can I mind myself but the Combe, and you from the first, and I've always called you 'Grannie.' Sometimes I seem to see another face but that goes. You say I b'aint your child, but I've been stoned for being your maid, and the folks they call you 'witch.'

"Sure I've never seen ought as folks could call you that for, I shouldn't have been here now if I had, and may be you knew it.

But they say you killed Tamsin Bale, and Miss Fishley down to the shop, and there be other tales a-going round as are cruel and worse of the lady up to the Grange."

Her stopped a bit to catch her breath, and steady herself, for she was terrible worked up, poor maid, she almost felt sometimes as 'twas some other person speaking, and not her at all.

"You've given me food, Gran," her went on, "and fire and a bed to lie on, and that I thank ye for. But no love, no nought but laughs and jeers, and they in plenty, and a bad name into the bargain.

"Now," her saith, clear and slow, a-working it off with her fingers, "What about Tamsin Bale? What about Squire's lady, and what about the little maid that was lost, Grannie, and has never been found to this day?"

Her stopped short sudden, for Nance had raised herself right up, and there was that on her face as made Malvina catch her breath and gasp.

Of all the evil human creatures Nance at that moment looked the most evil, her yellow face twitched and writhed, and her green eyes just glared, she tried to speak three times, and then her fell face downwards at Malvina's feet as one dead.

And Malvina was just terrified. Once before Nance had been taken something like this, but it weren't nearly so bad. She tried everything she tried afore, rubbing her, and putting brandy to her lips; but she lay there still where her fell with her eyes fixed. And the poor maid was near beside herself with trouble, thinking as Nance would die and maybe 'twas all her fault. 'Twas terrible lonesome for her with no person nigh to call and her daring seemed going right from her as quick as it had come.

Watching Nance close, at last she saw her eyelids flicker, then open, and shut quick, and her lips moved difficult. Malvina bent down close to hear what she was trying to speak, but the words come slow and thick.

"The Green bottle in the great chest," her whispered.

The great chest stood back in the corner where the shadow came, Malvina she'd never been there before as Nance had never sent her, and her always kept the key, but her knew as she had stuffs there as her gived to the folk around. She took the key from Nance's pocket and put it in the lock, but it took all her strength to lift the heavy lid.

There was rows and rows of jars, and bottles of all sorts, and bunches of herbs and snake skins tied together for drawing out blackthorn prickles, and packets of black cats' ears against the shingles, and things as her didn't know what they was, for her couldn't wait to see. But she found the green bottle at last and let fall the lid of the chest, locking it tight and taking the key to Nance.

Malvina poured some of the stuff in a spoon and put it to Nance's lips, and she scarce had swallowed it down, you may depend, afore the blood came to her face and she tried to raise herself up. But Malvina soon saw as the power had left Nance Darvel's right side and for the time she was helpless as a baby.

"You must bide where you be, Gran," her saith, "for a bit, till I bring the bed in here and get you into it."

How she managed it she never quite could tell, for Nance was a heavy woman and 'twas a difficult business to lift her, but she got her in safe enough and 'twas warmer in by the fire.

All that Christmas night she sat there watching, tending to the fire, and giving Nance sips from time to time out of the green bottle, and seeing as her feet were warm. And as her sat there her thoughts came full and quick, and strange things filled her mind. How near had she been to the truth, she wondered, and would she ever be nearer? How good Jan Williams was, and the Squire, he too was kind. And Malvina blushed, and hid her face in her hands.

And so the long night passed and the dawn it crept in cold, and she rose up and opened the door and looked down the snowy Combe, while up the valley came the music of Withyford church bells a-pealing for Christmas day.

CHAPTER IX

THE SNOWSTORM, AND MORE BESIDE

TOWARD evening when the light was getting dimpsey, Malvina went outside to shut the fowls up. She'd given Nance some broth and left her pretty comfortable, she seemed to be rallying wonderful quick considering how bad her'd been.

The woolpacks were rising heavy up over the edge of the moors, and the air was still with the stillness that comes afore snow.[35] The Combe looked grey and cold, and terrible lonesome and wist. Far above in the sky the wild geese cackled flying, while across her path as a moving ghost, a fox slid softly away; it was after the fowls, and good she came when she did.

Then the moon rose high above the crests of the woolpacks, edging them all with trimmings of light as shone, and the river below gave back the same as it ran.

And the lonely maid stood still, and sure her thought on her loneliness.

But I tell you 'twas twenty-four hours afore the snow came down and then it was only a blunk or two and waiting a whiles between.[36] But Malvina saw by the sky as there was plenty more a-coming, and she knew she was out of flour and things and fear'd a storm that might keep her to the house for days. So she made up her mind she must get to shop, afore it came on worse.

She put Nance to rights and made all haste, pulling on her scarlet cloak and hood against the rough weather, and taking the lidded basket.

---

35 Woolpacks: masses of fleecy white clouds.

36 Blunk: a flake of snow.

The heavens looked ready to fall as she hastened down the Combe. Now and again a big blunk fell and clung against her cheek, and she saw as the snow was not far off, from the way it was making ready. And sure by the time she came to cross lane it was falling soft and thick.

When she came to Liz Fishley's, if she weren't out of flour! and she had to wait till Liz she'd sent a boy to the mill, and Malvina worried much to think how the time was flying, for each moment the sow fell thicker and sure it was properly blinding.

When she rose up to go home, Liz Fishley never asked her to sit and wait a bit till it was over; not that I reckon Malvina would have anyway, for 'twould have meant all night, and Nance she couldn't be left. Though she felt, poor maid, as if she might never get home, and no wonder!

But she battled on bravely and got under the lee of the hedges, but the snow it whirled everyways, blinding and almost choking, and sometimes her had to cover her face to fetch up her breath to breathe.

She'd got her head well down, and was pushing bravely on, when someone suddenly jumped over the hedge by the linhay and knocked right against her.

It gave her a bit of a fright, and she started back with a cry. She could only just make out a man with a gun, for the snow was in her eyes, and that a dog was snuffling about her heels, and whimpering as if he knew her.

"This is no weather for women folk to be out!" and the man peered into her face, and she saw as 'twas the young Squire up to the Grange, and old Towler as always followed him.

"Malvina, it's surely you!" he saith, and stopped right up before her. "You can't go on in this weather, maid!"

"I must," she answered back, "Nance Darvel she's lying ill alone, I must get on afore it gets worse." And she took a step or two fore.

"But, my dear maid," he saith, "you must listen to reason. You can't go up the Combe to-night, for the storm's coming down with a tempest. It's all a strong man can do to stand against it, let alone a slight maid like you. You'd best come back to Thirza and let the old woman be."

"I can't, sir," she saith, "I must go right on. If you please, will you let me pass? And kindly don't keep me telling, for 'tis getting worse while we stand."

"Then I'm blest if you go on alone!" he saith. "You'll have to put up with my company, maid, but it's a mad vake at the best."[37]

So they both plunged forward into the driving storm, the snow getting deeper and deeper, while old Towler kept close to their heels, as he zimmed 'twas the easiest place.[38] 'Twas all Malvina could do to bide on her feet at times, for the snow it balled in her shoes so, and near threw her down. But the young Squire kept to her pace and to her side, stopping when she stopped, and getting before her for shelter when the storm got too much for her, and it came she was bound to wait to fetch up her breath to breathe. And so 'twas, till they came to the Combe, where the storm spun terrible swift.

"Malvina," the young Squire saith, "Do you still mean to go on?"

She scarce could hear his words for the drive of the wind. She had turned her back to the drift and covered her face with her cloak, but for answer, she dropped it again and battled on once more.

---

[37] Vake: piece of business.

[38] Zimmed: thought.

He'd taken her basket since they met, for 'twas cumbersome with the flour, and real heavy to carry, and now he took her hand and led her like a child. His ways were masterful and firm, and however much of her way she had got, Malvina she knew 'twas the last of it. So she just gave herself up to his guidance, feeling her own weakness; and she thanked the Lord that a strong arm and a steady heart was by to see her through with it.

So he held her up when she stumbled in the drifts, and lifted her when she fell; while the whole Combe was filled with the driftings and whirlings of the snow, and howling of the great wind which drove it back and forth.

'Twas so they struggled on, till Malvina was near spent, and till they came to the crooked thorn-trees round about Nance Darvel's cottage, where the going was easier, and they were under the storm a bit, with the drift coming gentler to them.

Malvina stood on the steps of Nance Darvel's cottage and shook the snow from her cloak, then she lifted the latch and they both went in together, with Towler at their heels.

But cold as they were and chilled right through with the weather, a sight met their eyes on entering which made their very blood freeze.

Nance was half up in bed and a light was full upon her, but it was not the light of candle or hearth, for the first there was none, and the second was only just living.

She was leaning fore on her elbow, gazing hard at the wall, and laughing soft to herself, and mumling with her lips. Sure 'twas an awful sight as froze the blood in their veins, for her face was the face of a corpse, with her grey hair hanging loose, and her green eyes fixed and dull.

On the wall beyond her was the shine and glow of a light that was neither of earth nor of Heaven, but I wager most likely of hell; for it shone on her awful face and her hand as clutched the bedclothes, and there was never a flame nor a flicker, nor a sign of mortal touch. And steady and clear in the midst looked down the face of the Squire; not the young one as stood so near, but the old one up to the Grange.

Since the two had opened the door, she had never once turned to the click of the latch nor the noise of their entering, so lost her was in the evil thing she was doing.

Malvina her felt half dead with fright and the Squire made never a move, but kept tight hold of her hand watching Nance as she did, while Towler slunk to their heels with his tail between his legs.

Nance she kept mumling low and laughing soft to herself, and all the time her seemed telling to some person a long ways off. But they couldn't catch what she said for her voice came strange and dull.

Sudden her laughed out shrill and loud and flinged her arms up high, "Squire! Squire! Squire!" her called, and each time it was more like a scream. "Ha! ha! I've made ye come, and once again I'll see ye and then on your bended knees; for you've something to ask old Nance as no other person can tell ye." Then she laughed and laughed again, and 'twas awful to hear her go on.

At last she made signs with her hands, moving them back and fore, and the light faded soft away and all the room grew dark.

Malvina drew her hand from the Squire's (though her could scarce breathe for fear, poor maid), then struck a light and went over and looked at Nance. She seemed deep in a heavy doze with no knowledge as folks were by, and her face looked terrible wan by the light of the dip.

"She's asleep," her saith to the Squire, "if you'll please to sit and warm yourself I'll make up the fire, that is if you b'aint afeard to bide in a witch's house."

The Squire leaned his gun in a corner and sat down on the settle, while Malvina put some fuzz to the ashes and blew with the bellows, and soon the fire it blazed and roared up the chimney; for 'tis a strange thing with turf ashes how long they keep the heat.

Malvina, poor maid, she was filled with dread and a terrible shame, and she crouched there on the hearth just a picture of despair, while the damp from her long dark hair, as had fallen loose through the storm, steamed round her like the mist in May, as rises afore the sun doth.

She knew now as the Squire telled for certain that Nance Darvel was a witch and no other, and what the folks said to Withyford was truth, and sure he'd class her the same and never believe in her more. How could he? seeing what he had seen, and knowing her lived with Nance.

She sat there with her cheek in her hand gazing into the fire, while the thoughts that were in her heart they moved across her face.

The Squire he just leaned forward and took a strand of her long damp hair in his hand. Soft and dark it was, and curling at the end, and moved like a living thing as he slipped it through his palm.

Malvina her felt the stir of his touch through her veins, as the breeze creeps over a field of corn afore cutting, and she trembled where she crouched and hid her face in her hand, while the Squire said never a word, but just softly coaxed her hair.

And so they sat while the wild storm howled and raged without, and within the firelight danced on rafters and hanging herbs, and played on the bed and curtains where Nance Darvel was fast asleep, and over the man and maiden and the shadows of her hair.

With one quick movement Malvina caught her hair and twisted it all together. The Squire leaned back in his chair and watched her coil it up, and when she'd done she sat there still but never looked to his face.

"Maiden," he saith at last, "I want to ask you something. You must try and answer me clearly, my dear, because it means a great deal."

Malvina knew he was leaning over her with the light a-catching his curls, and his blue eyes soft and tender; but for all that her dare not look to his face, but sat with her head bent low.

"How long ago was it, maid, before you came to live with Nance Darvel? And can you remember do you think, where you were before you came here?"

Then Malvina rose from the hearth and looked him straight in the eyes. He had broken the silence and with it her strange fears seemed gone, and she felt she might breathe again. He had given her a chance to tell him all and tell him all her would, and a beautiful maid she looked as she stood before him, a beautiful maid and one as couldn't lie.

"Believe me or not as you like," her saith, "but sure as I stand afore you; never once has Nance Darvel shown me ought of her doings afore. Why she had kept them from me is more than I can tell; but her has, and that's truth, as sure as I be a living maid, I know nought of her wickedness.

"No, I can mind nought afore I came here; maybe a woman's face, but that goes. Nance her's been kind in her way but always terrible close; and whenever I've asked her things she's always put me off with a laugh, and 'you're a lady my dear, a lady,' till I've been wearied to death of her talk. Every person her hates, sure love her has for none, but 'tis deadly hate her bears to Squire and all to Grange.

"I mind 'twas the night as the children set on me down to Bill Smiths, and Thirza took me back to Grange, and bound up my head. And when I came home, I told Nance all as had happened, and how Thirza wanted me to help in the kitchen. And her flew into such a rage as I'd never see'd afore, saying as she'd see me dead, 'fore such a day should come to pass. All at once she stopped, half closed her lids and thought; and when I went to Grange, she never said me nay. Maybe she knew I'd made up my mind, for Thirza's sweet ways had taken me, and she couldn't have kept me back if her tried, unless her'd used foul means.

"But that her hated the folk to Grange was no secret. Her curses were deep and dark on you all."

All through Malvina's talk the Squire sat watching her every movement. As she stopped, he rose up from the settle and took two or three quick paces up and down the room, and then stopped short in front of her.

"Let her curse," he saith with a quick fling of his hand to where Nance Darvel lay. "Let her curse! Malvina my dear, with the help of the Lord, we'll outwit her yet. What a life!" he saith half to himself, "What a life! alone in this Combe with that hag. A lonesome life and a sad."

"Aye lonesome and wist," she cried, and the tears come with a rush to her eyes, and her turned round quick to the fire to hide them. For her was a proud maid, and not given that way. He came and stood beside her and turned the log with his boot.

"I'd like to carry you right away," he said, "yes my maid, take you back to Thirza. But that old devil there can't be left, and no one but you would go near her."

"I told her the night her was taken ill, as I'd leave her for good and all," Malvina saith, "that is if she wouldn't tell me all she knew. But how can I now? I was going far away, long ways across the forest. Since the night to the Grange, I felt I could stand it no more, and I'd rather go amongst strangers and starve, than be so treated again."

The Squire stood there a bit, looking into the glow of the turfs, then he laid both hands on Malvina's shoulders, and turned her round so that he looked into her face.

"Promise me this, my dear," he saith, and she felt his strong frame tremble, "promise me this; that you won't run away dear, until you see me again."

The maiden stood silent beneath his touch, then raised her eyes to his, while the red blood rose to her cheeks.

"I promise you, Squire," her saith.

Then he took up his gun, and went out into the night, and Malvina was left alone.

CHAPTER X

MOTHER'S TONGUE MAKES TROUBLE

MOTHER and father were waiting up for the Squire that night. They was getting a bit anxious, for the snow kept falling steady, but still they knew he was out with his gun, and maybe he'd taken shelter at the Bartin, as he'd gone that way about.

'Twas getting lateish, when at last he came in covered with snow from head to foot, and properly numb with the cold. Mother got him as quick as her could into dry clothes, and made him drink a glass of herby tea, for there b'aint a better thing to drive the cold out than that there, you may depend.

The Squire spoke nought to father of where he'd been through the storm, and mother saw straight that there was something on his mind; for she knew every look on his face, and near each thought in his head, having studied him so since a child. So she got father off to bed, and bided to hear him speak, and sure after a bit it came.

"Thirza," he saith, looking across the hearth to mother, where she sat still knitting, "Thirza, that woman's a damned witch, if ever there was one."

And mother, her knew where he'd been, but still her said nought, knowing as more was to come.

He lay back in his chair, in the blaze and warmth of the fire, and the light brought out the red of his face as was caught by the storm, and lit up the gold in his hair; and sure he looked a splendid man as ever trod shoeleather, and mother her thought 'twould be a dainty maid sure enough, as would ever say him nay.

He was thinking out something in his mind, that mother could see, by the line in his brow, and the way he looked deep to the heart of the turf ashes; but she knew if her waited patient, sure she'd get it all by-and-bye.

Sudden he leaned fore to mother, "God's sake! Thirza," he saith, "who *is* Malvina? Now, 'tis no good your telling me she's that fiend's daughter, for I'll never believe it. She's made of different metal to that hag. I'll swear she's a good and lovely maid, and the Lord keep her, for she's in a queer place."

"Aye that her is," saith mother.

Then his face flushed deep and red as he told mother most all that had happened that night, of the terrible sight he had seen, of the awful look on Nance's face, and the light as shone that no mortal hand had struck, with the Squire's face plain as life, biding there, looking down, till Nance Darvel, her told it to go.

Mother she scarce could breathe for fear, as he told her of that night's doings. The wind kept making strange noises in the shutters, and sounds seemed to come from the dark corners, as she hadn't heard afore.

"Now Thirza," the young Squire saith, "you must help me to find all this out, for get to the bottom of this mystery I will, and nought shall stop me."

"Find out what? dear heart!" saith mother, almost too feared to speak, for she'd got that feeling as some person was behind her chair and her daren't look round to see. "Find out what?"

"Who Malvina is," he answered back, "and the meaning of the Squire's face up there, and the words Nance Darvel spoke this night."

Mother, she looked straight at him, and he at her; and there was two things as her read in his eyes and the tone of his speaking. One, and the first, that the strength of his man's love was given to the witch's maid, and no one could take it from her, and the other——

"Lord, Lord," her cried, sinking back, and near fainting with fear, "*That*, never, *that*, never *the little maid! never!*"

Mother, she sat and stared for a bit. Her was so taken aback by what her had heard, 'twas all she could do, poor soul. But presently things come back to her mind, things as had gone before, and the thought of Nance and her wickedness at the time of the lady's death; and one by one the things came back, and seemed clearer than before.

If Malvina was the maid, how could Nance have hidden her all those years?

How was it the thought never came to no person when Malvina first came back to the Combe, nor after. To be sure the maid had got at her heart from the first, and had ways with her, as weren't common ways, in spite of her bringing up.

And sure the old Squire had noticed something the night of the dance, and hard work her'd had to satisfy him, when he asked who the maid was; and putting him off with false answers, not liking to mention Nance. Maybe there was something he saw as minded him of the past.

Then mother, her saith, slow and steady, "yes dear sir, us must find it out."

"Is there any reason," the young Squire saith, "that Nance should hate my uncle, Thirza?"

"Never a one as I know by," her saith, "except the time he called her murderess, afore the whole of Withyford. And I reckon her made him pay strong for that, poor soul; for she witched him where he stood for all the folk to see."

And mother she went through all the story for the young Squire to hear, though 'twas many a time as he'd heard it afore, but this time he listened with new ears, I reckon, and a new understanding, putting questions to her from time to time, and making her go back over bits again, and when her'd finished, he sat for a long time silent, staring deep into the heart of the fire.

The storm howled round the house, and whistled through the shutters, and now and again came the soft, full rush of snow against the windows, and the hissing of it in the fire as it fell down the open chimney. And mother she couldn't help thinking, how terrible wild and lonesome it must be up the Combe, and of Malvina alone with Nance. So her thanked the Lord for a Christian fireside, and put on a log or two.

The young Squire got up and walked backwards and forwards through the kitchen, as if his thoughts had made him restless, and he couldn't bide still for them.

"Thirza," he burst out at last, "she's the little maid, I'll swear, aye, and I'll prove it too before she's many months older, though where that old witch kept her all those five long years, is what I can't make out."

"Dear heart, dear heart!" saith mother, "now don't you be too sure. You mustn't go setting your mind on this as if 'twas already come about. The Lord alone knows who Malvina may be and what wickedness Nance mayn't have been up to. The maid's a good maid and sweet, I know for sure; but don't ye go now and set your heart too much on what may bring ye to grief."

"Tut tut, old woman," he saith, "no need to talk of grief. 'Tis a wrong to be righted, more like, and I'll see to the doing of it, and what is more," he saith coming nigh, "you must help me Thirza, old woman."

He came to mother, and sat close against her chair, taking up her ball of worsted, and tossing it up and down. Mother see'd by the way he was setting to work as she'd have to give in to what he wanted, for she never could go against him when he put on them there ways.

"I want you to help me, Thirza," he saith, "but I can't quite make out how. I'd like to get Malvina right away, and bring her here to you, but that would set folks talking I reckon, and we must not do that. Then, whatever knowledge we get, it must come from Nance herself. I fancy the old woman's failing and she may let things out in her weakness, so it comes Thirza, I suppose, that nothing but patience will get us what we want."

And sure he looked just then, mother thought, as if patience would be the last thing he'd buy, and then he'd have a long price to pay for it, but her saith,

"That's so my dear! nought but patience. Now! I'll tell ye my belief. That Nance Darvel will never let her secret go till she comes to her end; but when that comes, be it soon or late, she'll send for the old master and tell it to him and no other, for whatever her's done, her's done it to spite him. You heard the wicked words that she spoke this night and you may depend as her'll carry them through. We must bide quiet and wait, dear lad, I'll see after Malvina, as much as the maid will let me, but I can't say as I'll go to the cottage, for iron chains shan't drag me there."

"I don't ask that Thirza," he saith, "No I don't want no living persons to see what I saw to-night, but 'tis that poor maid; I can't bear to leave her there. She talked of going across the forest as she couldn't stand the life in the Combe and Withyford any longer; but I made her promise," he saith with a flush, "to wait till she heard from you."

"Don't you take on about *her*," mother saith cheerful like, as it were putting Malvina on one side, "she's brave enough, the maid's a friend or two more now, than she ever had afore, and I reckon she's beginning to find it out. Now the kindest thing you can do, dear sir! (if you'll please forgive the liberty), is to leave the maid alone for a bit, and the harder you find it to keep away the kinder it will be. I'll see after her to be sure, you shall know what goes on in the Combe, I'll promise you, but you'll agree as I be a better caretaker of a young maid than you be, and maybe the Withyford folk will think the same."

Mother got up and bustled about the room putting things straight for the night; hoping she'd not said more than was wise to say, and that the Squire had seen what she meant. He'd flushed a bit at her words but said nought, and after a bit he came up behind her and kissed her on the cheek.

"Good-night old nurse," he saith with a smile, "your lad will do as you say." And mother knowing his ways felt as he'd bide by his words.

The snow lay deep on the ground another fortnight, too deep for mother to get about; but the first Monday she could she went down to shop thinking that she was pretty sure to meet Malvina there, and sure enough! just as she was leaving Liz Fishley's, who should come in but Malvina herself, looking a proper picture in her scarlet hood and cloak, though wan and pale, mother thought, but beautiful as ever. Soon as she saw mother her eyes lighted up and the colour came to her cheeks.

"Oh! Thirza," she cried under her breath, so as Liz Fishley shouldn't hear, "I be that glad to see you."

"I'll walk on down the lane a bit my dear," mother saith, "and as soon as you've done your business you follow on, for I've got a lot to say to ye."

When Malvina had got all she wanted she walked on quick after mother and caught her up just by Higher Cleve gate.

"How be you Malvina?" mother saith, "and how be Nance,

her's been really bad hasn't her?"

Malvina stared, wondering how mother'd got to know.

"The young Squire told me," mother saith, "same night as the storm, I wonder you weren't killed, out in such weather Malvina."

She looked sideways to Malvina, and saw the reds fly up to her cheeks, and her eyes drop, but Malvina her saith, "Nance be better, thank ye Thirza, but she can't walk yet."

"That be bad for you, b'aint it?"

"Yes 'tis bad," Malvina saith with a lift of her shoulders, "and I'd like you to show me something Thirza, as wasn't bad."

"Oh! I can show ye plenty," saith mother with a laugh, "you mustn't look through black, Malvina, but I reckon you were pretty well starved out that first week weren't you, how did ye get along?"

"I'd plenty of flour," her saith, "but I should have been pretty near I can tell ye, but for Jan Williams bringing me rabbits and such like."

"And did Jan Williams go to the Combe?" saith mother.

"Near every day since the storm," she answered.

Mother couldn't tell rightly how the feelings came, but she was just mad to think as Malvina was seeing so much of Jan Williams. 'Twas queer too, for at Christmas her'd have furthered it in every way.[39] But sure her was beginning to think in her mind of Malvina as "the little maid" and no other; and she felt as Jan Williams weren't the one to be talking and walking at all times with such as she. She thought on the young Squire, how mad he'd be to think of it, and with her too, for not keeping her promise to look after the maid and keep her in sight. So being angry with herself her turned it on Malvina, (a way mother had) and spoke with a sneer in her tone.

---

39 Furthered it in every way: put it out of her mind completely.

"I'd say you are well off for friends, Malvina."

Malvina looked up at once, both quick and proud, catching hold of mother's sneer. "I value all those as be friends in need and true," she saith with meaning, "but they that speak fair, b'aint always that." The red came bright in her face and stayed there, and mother, she fancied 'twas a snack at the Squire, as he hadn't been near her since the storm.[40]

"I reckon that us will be hearing wedding-bells to Withyford afore long, shan't us, Malvina? Let me know in time, my dear, as I may get a gown against the day."

A frown came in Malvina's brow, mother her wouldn't take warning, but went on, half-laughing, half-sneering.

"You'll make a handsome couple, but what'll Jan's father say to it? And there's Joan, poor maid, and the patterns got for her wedding-dress, why, I heard that a long ways back through Liz Fishley down to the shop, and she *did* say the colour 'twas, but I can't mind that, anyways you won't hear the last of Joan's tongue on your wedding-day, nor after it neither, that I'll warrant! And who'll the Bartin go to, I wonder? For Jan he'll ever have it. Be you going to live to Witches' Combe, Malvina?"

I reckon as mother scarce knew how stinging her tongue had got, she was so put out about Jan and Malvina, and worried with the way things had gone, not seeing her way plain through them, and knowing the Squire's thoughts. So I suppose she couldn't help but show her rubbed side outwards, and fretting Malvina with the edges of it. But when Malvina drew herself right up straight as a young larch, and looked at mother from head to foot, she saw quick enough then, bless you, as her'd gone a bit too far.

---

[40] Snack: a sneer or cutting remark.

The Snow Lay Deep on the Ground,
by Gratiana Chanter.

"Now Thirza," Malvina saith, "you can go back to Grange, for no person, not even you, shall sneer at me like that. But I'll tell you this for your asking and those as wants to know, that you'll never hear my wedding-bells to Withyford Town. When they ring, they won't ring here, none of your ears shall hear them. You can go, Thirza White," and she stood in front of mother and pointed down the road.

'Twas then mother found the old Squire's look in her eyes, and heard the old Squire's tone; and she felt shamed and cowed where she stood as if 'twas the old Squire speaking; and she stayed where she was, dumbfounded, as the truth it came upon her. Then, as if she walked in a mist, her went back through Withyford Town.

After that she was terrible uneasy in her mind to know what was best to do. She feared every day as Malvina'd be off with Jan Williams, and yet her knew as the maid would never leave the Combe so long as Nance was so bad. Then she'd no means of finding out how Nance Darvel was getting on, nor of Malvina's doings, except that she still came regular to the shop.

Another thing that troubled mother was how to satisfy the young Squire; for she daren't tell him as she'd had any difference with the maid, and yet her had to let him think that she knew all that was going on, and the deceiving of him troubled her, for her was always a straight one to act was mother, and had no liking for crooked ways.

That Malvina who lived to the Combe, and the little maid that was lost, were one, she now had never a doubt, since the look that had flashed to her from the maiden's eyes when she ordered her back to the Grange, and her didn't know what to do.

For she still kept to the thought as they must wait for Nance to tell, and that any over-hastiness might keep the truth from showing, and they'd be kept in the dark forever and the right be never shown.

So she said nought about her difference with the maid, keeping the young Squire off with what she thought best to say; and he believed her word, and that she had the maid in her care.

At last mother made up her mind as she'd set a spy on Malvina's doings, though who, she couldn't think; for looking round, there weren't one as she could trust, till sudden one day as it were she ran right up against him, no other you may depend, than that poor mazed creature, Tom Fool.

He'd been always terrible taken up with Malvina, ever since she came to Grange, fetching and carrying for her like a dog and hanging on all her words, same as he did to the Squire. And when she no longer came he wandered about as a creature who'd lost something, asking every person he met when she was coming back.

One day he came to mother with a blue string off Malvina's apron in his hand, laughing and singing to himself, as happy as might be.

"Now, where've ye been to," saith mother, seeing as what he'd got hold of.

"Up under the thorn-trees," he answered back, "the thorn-trees up in the Combe. Her hangs 'em up to dry for I've seen them and I know. They was wet and smelt of soap, Thirza, of soap, and the wind it blew high, and blew them against my face, 'twas soap, Thirza, sure!"

"Aye, aye," saith mother, "I reckon it was. Malvina's a good one for soap. Was her washing there all alone now?"

Mazed Tom looked up to mother, the vacant look coming into his eyes; and putting his head on one side he sang soft to himself, till her thought he never would stop, "all alone now, all alone now," and she saw as his mind had gone wandering.

She tried to take the strings from his hand, and that brought him back to himself.

"I stole it from the thorn-trees," he whispered soft, "I cut it with my knife. He was asking her to go across forest with him, but her shook her head, and said, not yet. I was against a great white sheet with a hole in it. I peeped through the hole and saw her quite plain. Her shook her head like this here, so."

"And never saw ye all the time," saith mother. "You be a clever man, Tom, after all, cleverer than most, for all the folks may say. Now, I want ye to watch Malvina, and see as Jan don't carry her off; us can't do without her, you know, Tom, and that's certain sure. You must hide as the rabbits do, and blink between the grasses, but never show yourself when Jan's about, or he'd soon drive you off."

"Hide, hide," he shouted out, "sure I can hide with the best of them. But," he saith low with a shiver, "I don't like the Combe when it's dimpsey, Thirza. I can't go *then*," he saith, "not *then*. 'Twas once mind," and a puzzled look came into his eyes, and all his thoughts went from him, and he burst out singing an old song as father sang at the shearing——

"There was a wealthy Squire who
Oft came her to see,
But still she loved her ploughboy
On the banks of sweet Dundee."

and mother see'd as he'd done with sense that day, and it weren't no use her telling with him any more, as all she'd put in his poor mazed brain would fall right out again. But she reckoned he'd watch all right.

So he did too, and brought her news of Malvina's doings to the Combe. How Nance kept much the same and Jan Williams was up to the thorn-trees, nigh every other day. The first she told the Squire as if it came straight from the maid, but of the last she said nought, knowing 'twould anger the Squire, and maybe, in his haste he'd undo the very thing he'd give his soul to prove And she knew as long as Nance Darvel was sick, Malvina she'd bide in the Combe, nor would she marry Jan Williams without leaving Withyford first.

CHAPTER XI
THE FLOOD

'TWAS so the winter went by, and the spring it came with the melting of snows and the sound of rushing waters.

Not in fifty years had the folk of Withyford seen the water so high. It carried away the bridge at Fordacre turn, and the low lying meads was all to a swamp and too soft for the cattle to feed in. Higher up in the moor it rushed in a mighty torrent, for the banks were steep and rocky with no place for it to spread.

It happened one day, when the river was at its highest, that Malvina went down to fetch up a load of water. She put her wooden pitcher down and stood watching the torrent afore her, and the rush and the roar of it so filled her ears, that her never knew that Jan Williams was nigh, till his hand was on her arm, and he saith close to her ear——

"Any person as tumbled in there wouldn't have much of a chance, would they, Malvina?"

"Not very like," she shouted back. "I saw a drowned pony colt go by just now, tossed along on the top just the same as if 'twere a straw. One can scarce believe 'tis the little Combe stream as goes tinkling by in the summer."

"Come back a little ways," he saith; "us can't hear ourselves speak." He took her hand, and they went and stood 'neath a bunch of withys a little way off from the stream.[41]

They stood a bit so, watching the yellow rush and toss of it, till Jan's eyes were drawn toward the maid Malvina, and sure he

---

41 Withys: willows.

didn't see nought else but her.

And she, I suppose feeling as 'twas so, dropped her eyes to the rushes at her feet, and the little wet places as showed above the turf.

"I can't wait, maid, I must speak now," he saith.

"Oh don't, Jan."

"I will, Malvina, you told me back in the winter that I must wait until the spring afore I spoke again, afore you could even think of it. You know what I mean, maid."

"Yes, Jan," she saith low.

"I've been terrible patient, Malvina, sweetheart, but, 'fore God, I can't bide any longer in doubt. I'm fit for nought with all this waiting about, and burning to hear you say, Jan, I love ye."

The strong hand that held her's trembled, and Jan's face was earnest with love, but Malvina she did not say the words he wanted, but still looked down to the rushes at her feet, and made a bit of a splash in a little pool with her shoe.

Jan drew her by both hands towards him and tried to kiss her on the cheek, but she wrenched her wrists free and put up both her hands against him.

"You shall not touch me," she saith. "The spring's not come yet, Jan; no, not yet."

"You're mocking me, maid," he saith, "you're putting me off. I'm sure I've been patient and studied you all that I could. Nance is no worse than her was, you could leave her now as well as later; now just you hearken, dear maid," he saith, and made a move towards her.

But Malvina took a step back and held up her hand.

Many's the time she'd kept him off like that before, but it weren't so to-day, for before she knew where she was he'd got her close in his arms, apouring out all he'd yearned to say, as warm as any sweetheart. Sure his love was terrible strong and true; and sure Malvina knew it now; for he held her to him as he could never let her go.

"My dear! my beauty!" he cried, "I love ye, I love ye," and he kissed her again and again.

Sudden a gun went off up over the Cleve, and the sharp barking of a spaniel come to them on the breeze.

"Let me go, Jan, let me go," her saith; and she slipped through his arms, and stood a little way off with a troubled look on her face, and her breath coming quick and fast.

"You'd no right to do that, Jan!" she saith with an angry light in her eyes, and a stamp of her foot. "I've told ye all along as I can't care for ye that way, and 'tis your own fault if you won't understand. Oh! let the marrying go, Jan, and just stay by me, sure! I don't know what I shall do if you won't."

"No," he saith firm, "I won't, Malvina: I've played that game too long for my own peace, and I can't do it no more. You must either go across forest with me, or I'll leave ye behind in Withyford alone."

The tears came in Malvina's eyes and her lovely mouth it trembled.

"You're hard, Jan," she saith, "but that you was kind I don't forget; when other folks left me you stood by—no, I don't forget. But you're going now, and in anger."

"Oh, Malvina!" he cried, "why won't you come?"

"There's Nance," her saith, "you know as well as I her can't be left. 'Twould be a sin if I did, Jan, and you know it, and there's no one else as would go nigh her."

"Try Thirza," he saith.

"No, never! Thirza's as hard as the rest. 'Tis no good, Jan, there's a bigger reason than Nance, as I've told ye, and as hard to get over. You must go 'cross the forest alone."

But a tear rolled down her cheek as she said it, and splashed in the pool at her foot, for she felt as her only friend was going right from her, and she could see no way to keep him.

Just then there came the bang of a gun again, and this time it sounded close above them.

"Who be it?" she saith.

"The young Squire, I reckon," Jan answered sullen. "I see'd him as I come along up over Lawny Cleve."

Malvina turned white to the lips. "I must be getting the water," her saith, and bent and took up her pitchers and carried them down to the stream. Jan stood where he was a moment, then followed her down and took the pitcher from her.

"I'll dip it up," he saith, "the water's running so swift it might pull ye in. Stand back from the river, maid, for the banks be rotten."

He scarce had spoke the words 'fore they heard a shrill scream from the cottage—they both turned quickly round; 'twas Nance at the door, and she not on her legs for the past three months. Startled they both were, as you may think, so much as Jan took a quick step back, and afore he could save himself, or so much as call out, he was battling for his life in the midst of the boiling flood, and tossed about like a last year's leaf and swirled away on its bosom.

Malvina stood as one turned to stone. It had happened so terrible quick, it near took her senses from her. But sudden the truth came, and she stripped the long cloak from her shoulders and ran alongside of the poor tossing thing in the middle of yellow flood as she knew was Jan Williams.

She hoped that the surge and swell of the current might bring him nigh her, so she held her cloak by the end to fling it to him;

but the swell and rush of the water carried him on with it, and she had to run to keep the pace it made.

Poor Jan was making hard battle for his life, but the rush of the stream over rocks and boulders was terrible. He kept his head up all he could, for he feared the stones more than the water, knowing a knock against one of them might put an end to him for ever. Every rock and tree he made a clutch at, the water dragged him off and turned him over and over, near stunning him with its noise. 'Twas like a cat with a mouse and playing a cruel game.

Malvina kept alongside, calling out loud for help, but her throat was dry, and her voice just hoarse with fear.

They were nearing a rocky fall with a deep pool at the bottom, which was now churned and seething by the weight of the water into it. Jan he was getting weaker, and she knew as no power on earth could save him when once he was in the pit, and if help didn't come before, why then sure 'twould come too late. She called out louder than afore, and prayed the Lord to save him, for it was terrible to see him so, with his drowning face and flinging arms, in the spin of the yellow water, that made her giddy to look to, and mazed with noise of its thunder.

Then a strange thing happened, which made her stop and catch her breath. Between her and the red-brown withys that grew above the fall she saw a man leap from the bank right into the yellow swirl. He caught a withy as he fell and gripped it like a vice, then leaned fore against the stream and waited for Jan Williams.

Jan's senses were most nigh gone with the buffeting he'd gone through, though, as he neared the withy bushes, he made one more effort to save himself, as knowing the fall was nigh, and gave one fling with his arms as brought him nearer the Squire. For sure 'twas no less than the Squire as had jumped in to save Jan Williams.

'Twas an awful minute, for the water was at its heaviest, but the Squire leaned fore with one arm free and the other tight hold of the withys, and as Jan Williams came along the swift sweep of the current, he gave a mighty fling forward with the arm as was free, and caught him by the middle. The pull on them both was terrible strong, and for a bit he had a fight for it; and sure it seemed for a time as both must go over the fall, for the water was like an evil beast, as it clawed and pulled them back, and sure Malvina thought 'twould claim them both for its own.

But the Squire's arm weren't as strong as a blacksmith's for nought, and inch by inch he beat the stream in all its anger and wrath with the help of the stout withy stems and the manliness that was in him.

Sure at last when he laid Jan Williams on the bank, Malvina her could have kneeled at his feet and kissed his hands where he stood, with the water pouring from his yellow curls, and dripping from his head to foot as a dropping well, he seemed, she thought, as an angel from heaven; poor maid, she was so thankful, though she scarce could tell if Jan were dead or alive.

Malvina bent down and wiped the mud from his face with her apron, while the Squire stood over her in the light of the cold March sun.

"What shall we do with him, Malvina," he saith; "he's no light weight to carry far. I reckon I'd better make haste to Bartin, and get some help from there, we're as near their place as yours, and the sooner he's out of this wind the better. Lord! it is cold. Rub his hands, maid, and watch him till I come. He's breathing right enough, but stunned, I think, and no wonder! that water was heavy enough to knock the soul out of any man."

He bent over Malvina, and just touched her on the head. "Don't be afraid while I'm away, my dear," he saith, and his fingers stayed a bit about her hair.

And sure, when he'd gone, the time seemed terrible long to Malvina. Her spread her cloak over Jan to keep him from the wind, which was blowing from the eastward, terrible cold and sharp. Jan never moved, but lay there white as a corpse amongst the rushes, with the grey light from the sky full upon him. And Malvina she kneeled there and prayed the Lord Almighty to save his life, feeling that through her, and those about her, he'd come to such a pass.

What could Nance have been doing of in the doorway, screeching like that, and she not able to put her foot to the ground an hour before: maybe the whole thing was one of her wicked tricks.

"Lord, Lord," she saith aloud, "what will be the end of it."

At last she saw the Bartin folk, with the young Squire along with them, coming down over the Cleve; and when they came up they cast side looks at her, and whispered among themselves, and she knew as they were tacking another sin to her door. They laid Jan on a gate, and wrapped him up in blankets, and carried him off, and the Squire was one of the number.

"Pick up your cloak, Malvina," he saith. So he left her.

And the maid went home with a heart as heavy as lead.

CHAPTER XII

HOW TOM FOOL BROUGHT NEWS

AS Malvina dragged herself home that night, there weren't a sadder maid to Withyford, nor a good ways round it neither. She felt all the world was against her, and life was a burdensome load, and she wondered much why the Lord had thought fit to bring her into it. She couldn't get the look of Jan's face out of her mind, tossed and scared on the heaving of the flood, not the noise of the water out of her ears, nor could she shake from her hair the touch of the Squire's fingers.

For his ways with her puzzled her sore, which, when she thought on them, brought the blush to her cheek, same as the night of the storm, and Nance's wickedness, when he made her give her promise not to leave the Combe.

Sure, months had gone by, and never since that night had he given her word or sign. There could be but one thing, that he believed what folks said against her, same as the rest of Withyford. But she'd rather he'd never crossed her path a thousand times, than he should have a chance to slight her. Still she felt the tingle of his touch upon her hair, and she gave just a shake of her head and hurried on up the Combe to get away from her thoughts.

When she reached the cottage she found Nance sitting by the fire same as usual. She said nought to her, being in no mind to speak of what had happened, and busied herself with the tay-things.[42] And when 'twas ready she turned and asked Nance if her should push up her chair to the table. But Nance gave no answer back.

---

[42] Tay: tea.

Malvina looked hard at her, and saw her open her mouth to speak, but no sound came from her. Then in a moment it came to Malvina that she couldn't, for her speech was gone.

Sure, the poor maid had had enough with the day's doings, without any more (though I suppose the back be suited to the burden, and sure her's was a young one), but 'twas terrible to see Nance silent, with a scared look on her face, as if at last the poor wretched creature she'd got something to put fear into her.

Then Malvina got scared, as Nance might die in the night; die with her there alone. She lit a light when the darkness fell, and took up a bit of sewing, but she scarce could draw her needle through with the feeling of fear as came over her. The place was awful still, save for Nance Darvel's breathing; sometimes 'twas loud and heavy, and then again it grew so soft that Malvina scarce could hear it, and she held her own with fear, in thinking that Nance was gone, and dare not look to the bed in dreading what she might see.

The whole place seemed full of fearsome things; the very herbs on the rafters were forming evil shapes; now growing long, then drawing back, then creeping, creeping, towards her.

She'd been too feared to make up the fire, but at last she got so terrorful, that she jumped up quick from her seat, and caught a bit of dry fuzz as was near her, and flinged it into the ashes. And sudden the place was filled with a dancing light, and the shadows grew short, and the black places were shown up.

Then Malvina crouched by the fire, and went over the day's doings, and so she sat near dead with tire and trouble, till the cold March dawn came up the Combe, and yellow streamers showed in the heavens above the crest of the Cleve.

Days went on, and Nance she grew no better. Her speech came back in a way, but not so ready as before. She kept to her bed, but her mind seemed always working, and her green eyes were every place at once.

Malvina saw no person all that time to tell her troubles to, or bring her news of Jan, which, poor maid, her longed for. Nor did she hear a word of the Grange or its doings; for whenever her went to the shop, Liz Fishley looked properly black at her, pushing the things she asked for at her, as if her was so much dirt; so she knew 'twould be no good to ask Liz Fishley questions, for if she did, 'twas sure she'd get no answer; and by the looks of the folks that passed her by, the maid could see that they laid Jan's drowning at her doors, and their faith in her as a witch was stronger than before, and sure her heart grew terrible haughty with the cruelty of their judgments.

'Twas one day not long after, she was sitting up by the thorn-trees. She'd just hung out some clothes to dry, where the sun shone warm, and the breeze played beautiful and fresh, when sudden she heard the call of the cuckoo, clear and loud, close to her. 'Twas hardly come April, and wonderful early, she thought, for it to be about. But it came again, loud and clear from the thorn-tree above her, and looking up quick, who should her see but mazed Tom mouthing and squinting at her through his long red locks, and chittering to her where she sat, 'midst the twisted arms of the thorn-tree.

"What be doing of up there!" she cried. "Come down at once, Tom, and tell me where you've come from!"

"I'll come down, Malvina," saith Tom. "I'll come down, to be sure, my dear! but I wouldn't have come when *he* was by; no, that I wouldn't, for all your asking. Why, Thirza saith I was to hide. Aye, hide like the rabbits! Sure I played "Hidy" well, *you* never saw me, Malvina!"

"No, no," saith Malvina, "I never saw you, but what did ye want to play hidy for?"

"Ha! ha!" Tom cried, while his eyes danced with mischief, "I know, but I shan't tell ye. *He* can't come now, he's bad in bed, *he* is. *He* can't carry ye across forest now, Malvina beauty; and that I know!"

"Be he very bad?" she asked, for she knew he was telling of Jan.

"Iss fye!" laughed the fool, "for they've got a doctor for him all the ways from Molton. I see'd him myself; he came on a black horse with one white leg to un. They say as you've 'witched' Jan, Malvina, for he doth nothing but call for ye from morn till night, and from night to morn."

"Oh, be he as bad as that?" cried Malvina. "Oh Jan, poor Jan!"

"I b'aint sorry," laughed the fool, shaking his ginger hair, and hitching himself from branch to brach of the old thorn same as a long-tailed squirrel, "I b'aint sorry, Malvina; I'm terrible glad."

Tom hung by a branch of the thorn, then dropped on the ground by her side.

"I'll tell ye why I'm glad," he saith, in a whisper. "I needn't come creeping up the Combe any more to watch him. There be pixies in the dimpsey here. I gathered their wool last year, a sackful down in the zug.[43] And Thirza saith they'ed be after me sure, if they caught me in the Combe, so I go terrible soft like, as they shan't hear me coming. Do you ever see them dance, Malvina, dance in the dimpsey, maid?"

"No, no," she saith, "you foolish Tom; but what did you watch and hide for?"

"Hide, hide," he saith soft, and the vacant look came into his eyes and his mind went off on a wander. He sat crouched at her feet, on a big grey stone, and she a bit above him, deep in a bunch of furze, as fair a maid as ever rested under the sun of heaven.

---

43 Zug: boggy or muddy ground.

"How be the young Squire?" her saith at last, and the colour flew to her face in the asking.

"He!" saith Tom. "Oh, Squire will be out to-morrow or next day. They won't keep he *in* for long. Iss fye! To-morrow or next day us will be up to higher Cleve after plovers' eggs; they'll be laying by now, I reckon, and Towler he's coming to. He's a fine one to nose them out, be Towler."

Malvina she asked him no more, for she'd got all she wanted. But she sat there still with her hands lying loose in her lap and her eyes on the track towards Grange. Her thoughts had slid a long ways off from poor Tom and his mazed chattering, while the shadows crept deeper and deeper up the steep sides of the Combe.

"The dimpsey's coming, Tom," her saith at last, "you'd best be getting home."

Tom jumped up quick and looked round. "Hush!" he saith, "they'll hear you if you b'aint quiet, Malvina. Don't you go and tell them now where I be gone to."

So he went off quickly across the Combe, walking soft and light, now quick, now slow, then stooping down and hiding for a bit, as if he really saw something and must wait till it was by. And Malvina sat and watched him till the dusk crept up and dropped as a mist between them, parting her from the only human soul she had to speak to.

And still she sat there 'mid the great Cleves of the moor; alone in the still silence and the gathering of the dusk; till the chillness which comes with it roused her from her dreams; her thought of Nance, I reckon, and maybe that the fire was low. So she rose up from the gorse and budding heath and stretched out both her arms.

'To-morrow! to-morrow!" her saith; "to-morrow, or next day!"

But the Combe was silent, except for the fall of water.

CHAPTER XIII

THE BROWN HAIR LISTENS

AND 'twas but the next day, sure enough, when Malvina was hanging out the clothes, that mazed Tom crept up behind her and sudden called the cry of a curlew sharp and shrill in her ear, near frightening the maid to death.

The maid turned round quickly with her hand to her side.

"Tom, Tom," she saith, "what be you up to, scaring a body like that there?"

Tom laughed a silly laugh.

"Ha! ha! I made ye jump, I reckon," he saith; "I made ye jump fine. Come with me, Malvina! Come! come! come! I've got them all in a hollow up over, two dozen or more, at least: they was cunning ones to find I can tell ye. Come quick!" And he caught hold of her hand and tried to drag her along with him.

"Stop still, Tom!" her saith, "bide a minute!" For he was dancing about, poor looney, as if he were on wires, trying to drag her up the Cleve to where he'd got his eggs hid.

"Stop still at once, Tom," her saith, "tell me, be you alone?"

"Alone, alone," he saith, with his vacant look and kind of singing. "Alone, alone, to be sure, alone."

"Stop your nonsense now, Tom," she saith sharp; "I'm not going with ye unless you're by yourself."

Tom stopped short and looked at her, squinting fearful through his red hairs.

"Lord, you *be* a looney, Malvina!" he saith as knowing as a judge, then burst out laughing as if he couldn't stop himself, and laughed, and laughed, and laughed.

Malvina saw that she'd get no more sense out of him, so as soon as he'd settled down a bit, she let him take her where he wanted, though her mind it partly misgave her.

'Twas a kind of hollow in the Cleve, a little ways over to the back of Nance's cottage. When the rains were heavy a spring burst there like a fountain, and made its way down over to the stream. But in the dry weather there was but a red scar in the brown Cleve to show for it, fringed along by the scented moor fern as grew there thick and beautiful. The sides were straight and deep, showing it had been a long time forming and for the water to have made so much way, and the heath grew wonderful high and thick, as a stag lying down naught could be seen but the horns of it.

As Malvina with Tom came to the edge and looked over, she saw on the other side, nosing about after rabbits and such like, old Towler up to the Grange; and a misgiving came over her as the young Squire was about, and she'd been brought to the hollow for something else than looking for plovers' eggs

"Tom," she said stopping short, "who else have you got along with ye!"

But almost afore her'd done speaking, the young Squire had raised his length out of the deep heath at her feet, and had taken off his cap with a "Good morning to you, Malvina," same as her'd been a queen.

The maid's heart beat quick, and she felt the colour leave her cheek, but there was that within her as bade her hide all passing thought from the man afore her, but her found it hard to do, for, in spire of herself, her heart gave great bounds, as she thought he surely must hear it.

She had made up her mind to one thing, that "Witch's maid" though he thought her, and worse, he should feel that her pride was as high as the greatest lady he knew, and play with her he should never.

And her proud thought let her meet the Squire's eyes steady and cool.

"I thought you'd like to hear that Jan Williams was better," he saith, "so I came here to tell you."

Malvina blushed and looked down, for she knew by the way the Squire spoke he'd heard of Jan Williams's courting. And the young Squire bit his lip as he watched her from under his brows.

"Thank you, sir," she saith; "I'm glad that Jan is mending."

"He's been as near death's door as a living man can be, Malvina. I wonder," he saith with meaning, "if it's glad or sorry he'll be to come back to life, maid?"

She made no answer, but colour came in her cheeks and burnt there, and her eyes flashed between the lashes.

"I expect you know pretty well, Malvina, which 'tis?"

Malvina raised up her lovely head and looked full at the Squire.

"Maybe I do," she saith, "and maybe I don't; but I'd say the best person to ask would be Jan Williams himself."

"So 'twould, only I thought maybe you could tell me as well, or perhaps a little bit better. For maids are changeable creatures. A man never knows what his fate may be when a woman holds his reins. A maiden's 'No,' so the world says, means nought, Malvina!"

All the hot young blood in Malvina's veins swelled up at his words, and she stood there up above him with a proud light in her eyes and scorn on her lovely mouth. She stood there against the blue of the sky, with the April wind from off the moor blowing the curls of her hair, and she looked a queen, as she stood there, for all her homely dress.

"And what may the world be saying," she asked, "of the truth of men's promises?" And she laughed a laugh as mocked.

They both stood silent; the Squire biting his lips, and kicking abroad a lump of turf with his foot. Malvina saw as he's caught her meaning, and she waited with flashing eyes to hear him speak.

"What kind of promises?" he said.

"What kind! well the kind you gave me the night of the storm; and the kind you made me give you. I've kept mine, Squire, what about yours?"

He just hung his head and looked down as the truth of the maid's words came upon him; and it seemed to him now false and cruel to have left her alone so long, and he was just mad with himself for letting Thirza persuade him to it. But how to tell her the truth: should he tell her? and risk all in the telling, as Thirza said he would. No, sure, he would put it off as long as he could.

"You've spoken the truth, Malvina," he saith. "You've kept your promise and I broke mine. I can't tell you why!"

"No," her saith, "but I can. On second thoughts, sir, you changed your mind. 'Twas safer to keep away from the witch's cottage, much more from the witch's maid; thinking the same as the Withyford folk, and judging her along with the rest."

The Squire turned white with anger, but his speech was still and quiet. "My dear, you've made a mistake," he saith, "and you'll know it some day."

"Some day?" her saith with a laugh, "oh. maybe, some day! Some day may be a hundred years hence, but *to-day* I know 'tis truth."

He took a step towards her and gripped her two hands tight. "You shan't say that again, Malvina; harm or no harm, you shall listen to what I say."

And before she could believe her ears he was pouring forth to her, as quick as his words would come, the story of the little lost maid, and how, from what Nance dropped that night in her wickedness, as Malvina was no less than "the little maid" herself, and that was his belief. And all that had kept him away from her was that the truth might come more plain to light, and that folks should have nought to say against her through his doings. And Malvina stood looking with scared eyes into his, while her heart-beats seemed to stop, and she felt she would fall where she stood.

"Let me go!" she cried, "let me go!" And her dropped down in the heather, and covered her face with her hands, for all as had come upon her seemed more than she could hold up against, and the moor and the sky seemed dim with gathering mists. But after a while they rose, and the truth it came upon her with a force as well-nigh stunned. And she was "the little maid." So she sat there silent a long, long, while with her face bowed to her knees. She heard a lark spring up to heaven and sing, and sing, till she nigh lost the sound, then drop down again ringing with song, and then stop. She heard old Towler barking away far down in the Combe below, and mazed Tom calling faintly after him. She heard the rise and fall of the stream as the breeze bore it upwards, with the scent of the March burnings in its breath, while it stirred the dark tendrils of her hair which lay against her cheek. Sure they all seemed speaking the same words:

"Good-bye, Malvina, and it's soon we'll be seeing the last of you."

Her heart swelled up with feelings which her couldn't check, and the tears came to her eyes and she burst right out crying, as though her heart must break.

"Don't, don't, dear maid," the Squire saith, "sure all will come right, now don't you cry," and he kneeled down by the side of her, and stroked her bent head soft.

But Malvina having once begun, sure her was bound to have it out, and she cried as maids will when things have been too much for them, and there's nothing else to do.

'Twas after a bit that the Squire's words and touch seemed to soothe her, and her sobs grew less, that she raised her head, and looked to him all through her tears.

"Will ye please to forgive me, Squire," her saith, "but how could I tell?"

"Don't think any more of your words, dear maid!" he saith, "you were right to speak as you did. But I could not stand still and hear you judge me falsely. I was bound to speak, whether for better or worse, the Lord only knows."

He took her hand and kept it, softly stroking it back and fore with his own, and they both stayed silent a bit with the noise of the stream coming to them. To Malvina the very moors seemed changed, and a light shone in her eyes, which, with all their brightness, had never shone there before.

"Dearest maid," he saith, "will you make me a promise! 'Tis for your good, child, or I wouldn't ask it. It'll seem a bit hard after what I've been saying."

"I'll promise," her answered low; "what be it?"

He looked deep into her eyes.

"You must trust me, maid," he saith, "trust me all in all. Will you, my maid."

Malvina looked back and held his eyes with hers.

"Yes I will," her saith, "I'll trust ye, Squire, through all."

"Kiss me then, Malvina!"

She lifted her face to his, and quick he had his arms about her, and their lips had met in one long kiss as sealed their love forever.

A brown hair came out and sat looking at them with his long

ear cocking back and fore. Maybe he thought 'twas good to see sweethearts about, as a sign that spring had come. The cloud shadows raced one another over the tops of the moor, as if at a game of play, making purple shades and yellow lights as they ran. Spring seemed everywhere, and singing a song for they two. And they let it sing, dear hearts, without knowing, for nought could they see in the world but the light in each other's eyes.

"I must go," Malvina saith at last, with a sigh, "I must really go."

He asked her to bide a bit longer, but her wouldn't, and they rose up from the heather hand in hand.

"Go back," she saith, "the way you came, and I'll go mine. I'll do all you say and bide quiet; and pray the Lord as Nance may speak afore it be too late."

He took her in his arms and laid her cheek against his breast, and looked down far into her eyes.

"Malvina, my darling," he saith, firm and tender, "I'll sware 'fore God, whatever happens, that you shall be my wife. Nance may be silent or speak; it makes no difference, you, or no other woman under the sun. Maid, you believe me?"

Malvina answered with her lovely eyes as full of trusting love as a June rose be full of scent; and again they kissed each other as lovers will, and sure as lovers shall to the end of time.

When at last they parted and Malvina had taken her way across Cleve and was once more in Nance's cottage, her scarce could believe as it weren't some strange dream come to tempt her in her loneliness, and sure her'd wake up and find it all untrue; and all as had happened out on the Cleve would melt away as the moorland mist and leave nought behind but the same black life which she knew.

But the place looked just the same, she thought, just the same, only different. Sure, there was the black crack over the fire, and the

The Brown Hare Listens, by Gratiana Chanter.

herbs, and the smoky rafters. And there was Nance with her evil eyes, watching her every movement. But there was that on her lips as thrilled her still, and words in her ears as rang and rang as the chiming of Withyford bells; and the world was changed with their ringing.

"His wife!" And a proud light shone in the maiden's eyes as she thought on the word, and a fresh spring came to her step, and she felt she could bear all that might come with such a love for her own.

Sure her'd be patient and wait. For Nance must tell that secret truth which she knew and no other. The truth which should raise her up to the height of the man who loved her, that his name should never be dragged in the mire, nor dropped in the sight of men.

And Nance Darvel sat watching her as she moved here, there, and everywhere, with a new light in her eyes, and a new spring to her foot.

"You've got a sweetheart, Malvina!" her saith. "And it b'aint Jan Williams."

CHAPTER XIV

NANCE DARVEL COMES BY HER END

THE thorn trees grew white with blossom and the blossom fell. Then June came along filling the lanes with honeysuckle bowers and strings of wild rose flowers and the scent of them hung in the wind.

The grass was down in the Squire's meads along the bottom; and sure, near every place you might hear the ringing of the scythe, and the even swish of it as the mowers bent their backs; from the rise of the sun till the dimpsey grew so deep that the folk could see no longer.

It was nigh the end of June that the weather came in terrible close and heavy. There was near a week of it with never a breeze, and the little there was like that from an oven door. Folks knew that the rain must fall afore the air could cool.

'Twas the Friday, I mind; when great clouds began to rise to the eastward.

All day long we heard the low mumbling of thunder far away out over the ways they came, and the air was wonderful still, as you might hear the sheep bleat easy as far out as six-acre field.

Mother was out in the dairy skimming cream off a pan. 'Twas just about five o'clock, and her was taking it off for tea, as father loved it dearly, when her heard the young Squire calling hasty from the outer kitchen door.

"Here I be, sir," she saith, "a skimming crame for tay."

He came quick into the dairy, his face was burning red and beads of sweat stood on his brow, and his breath came and went in panting gasps as though he'd been running hard.

"Lord! dear heart now! whatever be the matter?" mother saith, while a lovely bit of cream as her'd got on the skimmer slipped off with a splat on the floor, without so much as her finding out that 'twas gone.

"You must come at once! at once, with me, Thirza, she's dying."

"Dear heart and life! who?" mother cried.

"Why, Nance Darvel," he saith. "Put on your bonnet quick, woman; where's Squire?"

"Dear, dear! my blessing!" mother cried. "But you won't take he?"

"Where is he, Thirza?"

"Out under quince, to be sure," her saith, "as being the coolest place;" but he'd gone like a flash afore her'd finished speaking.

Mother got on her bonnet quick and took off her apron; being all to a flitter with thinking on what was coming: and a terrible dread of Nance and her end came over her, as she thought she could never go through with it.[44]

Her went to the door, sure there was the old Squire already on the mare with his face grey and drawn, and she guessed by his look as the young Squire had told him.

All the folk were down to the hayfields and there was no person about, so the young Squire had put saddle on the mare, and now was girthing up old Acty ready for mother to mount.

How her got up her could never think; but before she knew, she was following on after the old Squire with the young one holding on to her bridle rein.

They kept away from the village, going a cross cut down over Shallyford, and up over the track that ways to Witches' Combe; mother thought sure once or twice her'd be off, the Cleve was so

[44] All to a flitter: all of a flutter.

steep and the stones rolling away under Acty's hoofs in a way that terrified her. But with clinging on to the pummel with both hands, and the young Squire steadying her when they came to a bad bit, they reached the bottom of the Combe without much hurt.[45]

The heat was something awful, and seemed properly scorching, whilst the mutterings of the thunder came more and more nigh, and more frequent.

They rode silent, and spoke nought. The old Squire's head was bent low over his mare's neck, and his eyes seemed looking a long ways off at things which no other person saw. His reins hung loose and the mare just took her own way. Sure, mother said, it seemed a terrible long time afore they came in sight of Nance Darvel's cottage.

Then they crossed the stream, and the horses went stumbling over the stony track, 'twixt the heath that was purple with bloom, till they came to the crooked thorns.

The young Squire tied up Acty's bridle and lifted mother down, who was trembling from head to foot.

"Wait there, Thirza, with the Squire," he saith, "while I tie up the mare in the linhay, maybe there'll be some rain."

But he weren't gone two minutes 'fore he beckoned to them from the corner, and they followed him into the cottage where Nance Darvel, the witch, lay dying.

Propped up in bed, her breath was coming in quick, short gasps, and her thin fingers, like birds' claws, was clutching at the bedclothes. Her face looked terrible drawn and grey, and her eyes, sunk deep in dark hollows, flashed everyways to once as green as ever.

Malvina stood by her side, white as the apron she wore, but as the Squire came in she stepped back behind the settle in the shade.

---

[45] Pummel: pommel, the rounded knob or raised front of a horse's saddle.

The old Squire went straight to the bedside and looked down to Nance; while mother sat quickly down on the first chair she came to near the door, on account of the heat, and being that terrified, she didn't know what to do.

And the young Squire went over and stood by the side of the old one.

Soon as Nance Darvel caught sight of him her gave just one scream, and lay there gasping, with her breath coming terrible quick, as mother thought she was dying there and then. But after a bit it came quieter, and as she lay, her laughed softly to herself, and sure it was awful to hear.

"Ha, ha!" she saith, "I knew as you'd come; I knew I could fetch ye when I liked, Squire, and here you be."

"Woman," saith the old Squire, with his hawk's eyes fixed on her, "what do you want of me?"

"Ah, sure!" she saith to herself with a long sort of sigh, " 'tis sweet to hear him spake, sure 'tis sweet. Many's the times I've longed to hear him tell, many and many's the times, knowing all the whiles as 'twould be only once. And that's *now*."

And she lay there still some minutes, with only the sound of her breathing.

"Nance Darvel!" the Squire saith again, and his voice went solemn and clear through the room, "why have you called me here? If you have ought to say which may clear your mind of much wickedness, and give right to those whom you've wronged, 'tis best to say it now, for your time is short."

Nance listened to every word with her eyes upon him.

"Who'd have thought as I'd go before you," her saith; "who'd have thought it now? Why, you was struck an old man the day the lady died, your hair was white when you called me murderess afore the whole of Withyford—aye, white as snow in January. Ah! I do not forget—no, sure—how your eyes flashed hate; I loved well to see them so; you knew I'd taken the little maid, you knew it, you knew it. You'd have killed me where I stood if I'd let you, Squire."

There was a deep silence after she spoke, save for her laboured breathing. Mother saw the old Squire's hand open and shut on the bed post. He was being terribly tried, but that Nance must say what she'd got to, and in her own way, or may be she wouldn't at all, was what they had to bear with.

A peal of thunder broke above the Cleve, and rumbled away out over. 'Twas growing darker every minute, and mother could see as drops was falling, leaving dark rounds on the door-step outside, and showing the storm was nigh.

"I hated her," Nance gasped out. "I hated all you loved," and then her waited a moment. "Stand to the bottom of the bed, Squire," her saith; "I can't see ye where you be; stand where I can see ye, the light falls fuller there."

The Squire moved as she said, and leaned on the wooden bottom of the bed.

"Once," her saith, " 'twas three year afore she came, and on May day, as you kissed me in the ring. You thought naught, but you had my soul along with it. Next year you danced with me twice; 'twas up to Bartin shearing. I heard you call me a handsome maid. And I loved you more than my soul."

A lightning flash lit up the room, and a peal of thunder burst after it, as made the whole Combe echo.

Mother went across to Malvina and took her hand, for the poor maid was crying.

"You gave never a thought to me," Nance went on; "no, never

a thought to me; your dogs fared better far, it made me mad; but I hoped, sure I always hoped, till she came. Then, then," her cried, gasping and shrill, "I sold myself to the devil one day, so as I might be your ruin."

A lightning flash came again, as blue as a bell, lighting up the whole place, with a peal of thunder as rolled and echoed from hill to Cleve, as if it would never stop, drowning Nance's voice whenever she tried to speak. Then the rain came down like a water-spout, and poured and ran from the fern thatching in streams.

"I sold myself to the devil," Nance saith low; "that's sure enough, but I b'aint going to say *how*, for that's my secret—sure I've many. I tells what I want, but no more."

"Malvina," she called, "go to the old chest there, and you'll find a little box in the corner, locked. The key be on the bunch, bring it here, maid."

Malvina came fore trembling. Her tried for the lid, but her eyes were so full, somehow she couldn't get at it, and the young Squire seeing how 'twas, came over and lifted it for her.

She stooped over the chest and groped about feeling for the box, but she couldn't find it no place; there was a smell of herbs and dust, and she half feared what her might come against.

"To the left," Nance cried impatient. "To the left, maid, I'll stake my life it's there."

And sure enough Malvina fetched out a black oak box with a bit of a carved lid to it, and a lock, so she took it to Nance with the key."

"Open it," saith Nance, "for I can't"

Malvina scarce could fit the key in the lock for the trembling of her hands, and when she got it there her couldn't turn it, till the young Squire leaned over and twisted it for her.

"Open it, maid," saith Nance, "and take out what is in it."

Malvina put the box on the bed and lifted the lid. First come a wrapping of paper, and under that was some soft white stuff a-lying. Her took it out and shook it from its folds, and held it up to the light.

Mother, with the rest, had followed all Malvina's doings, but when she saw what Malvina held she came fore with a cry as her couldn't keep back. Sure the memories as came to her with the sight of what she held was more than her could bear without a cry.

"The little maid's," she called out, "the little maid's. Oh, Squire, Squire, why, I sewed it every bit myself, and the Mistress got the ribbons all the way from London. Oh Lord! Lord!"

"So you know it, you fool, do you?" saith Nance, in a husky whisper. "Mazed Tom he knew it too when he met her on the road, for he made a snatch and carried a bit of it back. 'Twas lucky I met him and settled him when I did, or those Molton gentry wouldn't have let me off so easy, for all my handsome looks." And she laughed huskily to herself.

'Twas a baby's frock as Malvina held, with the blue ribbons that tied up the sleeves all checked over with rosebuds. A deal of love and thought had gone into that little frock, you may depend. Mother knew every stitch of it, and that 'twas the very one the little maid had on the day she was lost.

"I laid my plans a long while back," Nance saith. "There was one as I knew would help me though. Her's dead and gone. I waited my day, and it came. You was out, Squire, and Thirza there, and nought was left to manage but that fool Liz. I put stuff in her drink, while she slept 'twas done, and the little maid was out of Withyford and across forest afore anyone could tell.

"Ah! they as had her knew how to hide sure enough. But I

plotted it all, and the lady were mazed by my help," she cried, "and the knowledge of what I had done."

The old Squire leaned heavy on the bottom of the bed as trembled under his hands.

"You devil," he saith between his teeth, "to tell me this to my face."

"Ha, ha!" Nance shrieked; "I've only lived for this; I've left you lonely all these years, and I've had what you'd have given your very heart-strings to possess. Yes, I've had it, Squire, not you; 'tis Malvina the beauty, Malvina the witch's maid. There her be, Squire, there her is! look to her."

She managed to raise herself half up in the bed, and bent fore with one skinny hand pointing to where Malvina stood leaning against the great oak chest.

"Her's your voice, Squire," her went on. "Many and many's the times I've heard you speak through her mouth, and loved her for the same, but her's her mother's eyes and ways, and there's been times I can tell ye as I could have killed her for them, for she be a fine lady to her finger tips for all she's lived to Witches' Combe."

The Squire he left the bed and went across to Malvina.

"I must look at you, maiden," he saith. He took her face between his hands, so as the light from the window fell upon it, and he stared long and earnest at every feature, but most to her lovely eyes.

"Margaret's eyes," he saith slow and tender, " 'tis true; my Margaret's little maid."

And he opened his great arms and gathered her gently to him, thinking on his lady so long laid in the earth, and deeper things, I reckon, as no person dared pry into, for God Almighty only knows the bottom to some wells, nor the shape of the stones as lie hidden below.

Then it came to pass as Nance was still leaning fore with her eyes upon the Squire, as if her saw nought else in the room, that the whole place was suddenly in a glare of blue light which seemed everywhere at once, and a noise broke over the roof as brought deafness to their ears. A more terrible thunder than they had ever heard afore, as burst right on them and shook and tore at the walls as to drag them from their very foundations.

Mother thought sure as the end of the world had come, and her flinged herself on her knees and prayed as loud as her dared, and hid her face in her hands, so that she might see nought. So her bided till her heard the young Squire call and the air seemed thick with the smell of singeing blanket.

"Good God," he cried, "the woman's struck."

Sure he spoke the truth, for Nance Darvel, the witch, lay dead on her bed, brought to her end by a lightning flash.

CHAPTER XV

THE WEDDING TO WITHYFORD CHURCH

SO Malvina's troubles were over at last, dear maid, though sure they called her Miss Margaret now; 'twas her mother's name, and somehow Malvina went with the Combe and her shame, and 'twas better left behind.

They took her up to London to the young Squire's mother, for her was still living though always on her back, poor lady. She kept Miss Margaret with her for nigh upon a year, to learn the gentlefolks' ways, their books and the such like, I reckon! Then she came back to Withyford a proper lady, and many weeks didn't slip 'fore there was a wedding to Withyford church.

Lord! how lovely she looked as she came down along through the folk; stepping the ground like a queen, same as she aways did, in her long white trailing dress, and the folks all throwing flowers. And mother she couldn't help thinking on the time 'neath the lilac trees when they'd other things to throw than roses and pansy blooms. But sure 'twas nought but flowers now to fling at the Squire's bride.

And the young Squire turned and kissed her on the steps afore them all, with his curls all shining yellow in the sun, a proper man to look to, and the old Squire turned and blest her where she stood. And all the folks set cheering as you hear for miles around, and hadn't been heard to Withyford since the Squire's lady came.

There was a dinner up to the Hall for all the folks in the place, and fine works mother had to see them married and get the food right too. The bells they rang all day till Johny Light he broke the rope and they were forced to give in through not being able to find no other, and being only three bells to start with, they couldn't go ringing with two. Though some say as Johny broke the rope on purpose, there being dancing up to the Grange and he being mazed for a jig.

And so life had come back to the Grange once more, and love to the old Squire's heart, for the young Squire's lady was all that a daughter could be, studying him every way with all the love she could give.

Jan Williams he left the place soon as he heard the news of the picture found in the black oak box. 'Twas a picture of the Squire's lady as fresh as her was in life, and when they placed it alongside of the young Squire's lady you'd have thought 'twas the maid herself. It was tied round her neck the day she was lost, and Nance kept it with the rest.

And poor Jan Williams, it all was too much for him, though Miss Margaret she wrote him a beautiful letter that I'll warrant he kept to his dying day, though letters be cold comfort when a man loves like Jan. And one day he sailed for the Indies, and no person's heard of him since.

'Twas another eight years afore the old Squire went home. The young ones had spent most of their time to Withyford going backward and forward to the young Squire's mother in London. But after the old Squire's death they went to her altogether, for I fancy, at times, as Withyford was a little too much for Miss Margaret, the life in the Combe and the past coming back too plain.

And Joan she married Farmer Blake as lives over Molton way. And Lord! they say he *did* have a life of it, what with her tongue and her temper. But the man was after her money, so I reckon it served him right.

'Twas death came to mazed Tom soon after the master went. He just "wanged" right away, grieving, I reckon.[46]

Father and mother stayed on to the Grange, and sure, as they lived so they died, with no thought but of faithful love to the Grange folk in their minds.

And the cottage up in the Combe it stood there till it rotted. Just as it was with Nance Darvel's bits of things in it. For no person dare go near nor wished for nought that was her's, thinking 'twould bring them no good, nor would it, you may depend.

For they who were doing the last by her found something behind the chimney as you scarce would believe was true, though the one as told me I know her weren't no liar.

'Twas a little wooden image stuck full of pins as a hedgehog be full of prickles, with a little thing on the top of it just like the old Squire's hunting cap. Sure 'twas one of her witch's ways, and some awful curse against him.

And it got about those who rode home late at night-times, as they saw lights for certain sure in Nance's window; sometimes 'twas a blue, another time 'twas a red. And awful screams that rang right up the Combe, and they reckoned as Nance Darvel had come back to haunt the place and the folks was more feared of the Witches' Combe than ever, and they was brave men or drunk ones as ever ventured nigh it.

But you may be sure, 'tis truth; as long as the moor blooms purple and the west wind blows across it; as long as the cold snow flies and the hay be cut in the meads, so long will the witch Nance Darvel be telled of to Withyford Town.

---

[46] Wanged away: yielded to exhaustion, faded away.

OTHER STORIES

'Appledore', by Gratiana Chanter, from *The Rainbow Garden.*

THE APPLEDORE BOY

From *The Rainbow Garden*, 1901.

WELL, he was called "The Appledore Boy" by most folks, though Betsy and old Bill called him "Jan," which means John at Appledore, and, indeed, in most parts of Devon. But no one knew who he was, or where he came from, or anything at all about him, only Betsy pretended she did, which will sometimes do almost as well. For, you see, this is how it happened.

One October afternoon the Appledore sailors stood about in groups on the old grey quay telling each other that "there'd be a storm before night, and they reckoned there'd be pretty roughish weather outside." The storm-signal had been run up on the yellow sand-hills across the river, while the bar kept up a steady thunder, which all the sailors knew meant mischief.[47]

The "Pool" was thick with the masts of ships lying there for safety, and the incoming tide bore vessel after vessel up to Bideford to refuge for the night.[48]

Ships from all parts of the world were there—from France, Italy, Spain, besides Welsh coal-boats, and the dear little Clovelly fishing-smack with her beautiful red sails.

There was an angry sunset, and the sky was stained with orange, crimson, and yellow. Great black clouds blew slantways, like swift black wings of wicked angels. The sea and the river grew dark, and the wind whistled and moaned through the rushes on the sand-hills.

---

[47] Bar: a build up of sand where a river or harbour meets the open sea.

[48] Pool: a wharf or quay.

In the night the storm came. The wind blew guns. The "Bar" leapt, thundered, roared, and flung into the air great fountains of white water. Out on the sand-hills the wind shrieked and screamed. The flying-foam and whipped-up sand were blowing. Indeed, it was a heavy storm.

But a storm, more or less, is not much to Devon folk, and the only thing which made Betsy distinguish this one from another was that the morning after, when she opened her door, seated on the doorstep, was "The Appledore Boy."

"It properly took my breath away," said Betsy to old Bill, the Ferryman. "My dear, you might have knocked me down with a feather. There he was, a proper little being, a-sat upon the doorstep as if he'd a-growed there; and when he put out his little hand and began to cry, now what could I do, man, but take in the poor chiel and give un a bit of meat?"[49]

"You couldn't do nought else, dear soul," said Bill. "You couldn't do nought else. If the Lord set un down at your door, I reckon he intentioned you should take un in."

So Betsy "took him in;" for, being a kind-hearted Devon soul, she could do no less. So you see that no one but Betsy knew anything about "The Appledore Boy," and she only found him on the doorstep the day after the storm.

But some of the neighbours used to say "Betsy knew more than she'd tell." For when they came to her with questions, she would say, "Folks might have their notions, she'd think, without sending Town-crier round Appledore with them!" But Betsy had no "notions," only she liked the folk to think she had.

"The Appledore Boy" was about two years old when Betsy

---

49 Chiel: child.

found him sitting on her grey stone doorstep. Of course he was too young to *say* much, so he spent most of his time sitting in the sun outside Betty's door, watching the rippling tides flow up and down and the vessels sailing by.

And what the "Boy" thought of at that time nobody could tell.

As years passed on the Boy grew older, but he was so unlike the other Appledore boys that people said odd things about him.

"I reckon the child's queer," said Liza Ann Rudd (Betsy's neighbour). "I reckon he's mazed, poor soul!"

But Betsy was very fond of Jan, and she was quite sharp with Liza Ann Rudd for calling him mazed, though Betsy often wondered herself why he was so different from other children. But she said, with her head in the air:—

"What do 'ee mean, Liza Ann?"

"Well, you see," said Liza Ann, "it ain't natural for a chiel to go on as he do. It ain't natural for a chiel to sit all day long and stare before un. What do un see? say I—what do un see?"

"I reckons he sees the ships and the river. There's not much else to see," said Betsy.

"Why don't 'ee send un down 'long with my Maryann out cockling? There's thousands down there in the mud."

"I tell thee he won't go, Liza Ann, and I've told thee so before. He will go 'cross ferry with old Bill, and look as pleased as a cappen; but never with the childern."[50]

"Iss; and ask such questions as no chiel ever asked afore! Mark my words, Betsy, that boy will *never* come to no good end. *My* belief's he's *witched.*

Now this made Betsy angry. For to say in those days that any

[50] Cappen: captain.

one was "witched" was to say a very offensive thing. So she told Liza Ann to mind her own business, and never spoke to her for a month of Sundays, though she lived next door.

And what did the boy see, do you think? Well, he saw just what Betsy said he saw—"the ships and the river." But he saw them with very different eyes to Betsy's or to Eliza Ann Rudd's. And, do you know, I do not think that he was a bit "mazed" to sit all day and watch the river. For, oh! it is such a silver, happy, gliding river. It told the boy such wonderful stories; and so did the graceful, shadowy ships. Some of the ships' stories were sad, especially after a storm. Then they would be towed up the river with their poor sides all torn and their slim, tall masts all broken and battered. The boy would feel so sorry for them. His great eyes would fill with heavy tears. Then the incoming tide would tell him "not to mind, for he was carrying them on to Bideford to have their poor sides mended and a new slim mast set up." And when the vessel came down again, whole, stately, and beautiful, think how happy the boy was!—for he loved the graceful vessels and the silver, gliding river. They were his friends, you see, because they understood him. They never thought him "queer," bless you! But then they had been far into the world, had the gentle ships, and knew so much—ah! so much—more about boys, and things, and places, than Liza Ann Rudd.

The "Appledore Boy" had one friend, whom he loved most dearly—old Bill, the Ferryman. For I must tell you that there is a village opposite little Appledore called Instow, and when the people wanted to cross the Bideford river, which divides Appledore from Instow, they always went in old Bill's ferryboat. And when trade was slack—that was, when nobody wanted to cross—old Bill would take the boy on the river a bit, and then what a time the Boy would have!

Nobody ever told such wonderful stories as old Bill. He had a story to tell of every vessel that ever dropped anchor in Appledore Pool; stories of shipwrecks, smugglers, and pirates; and of all the wonderful things the sea washed up; and of the beautiful things, and marvellous, that the fishermen found in their nets; and all about the mermaids.

"All about the mermaids?"

Yes, all about the mermaids. Now, I am well aware that some people hold there are no such things as "mermaids." But old Bill had seen them out by the "Bar," and the Boy saw them after. So it only shows how ignorant some people are, and what nonsense they talk!

As the Boy had a good deal to do with the mermaids, and the mermaids with the Boy, I had better push on with my story, and tell you all about them.

Old Bill told the Boy that years ago he had a little sweetheart—the prettiest maid in Appledore. One summer morning she went down on the sands with the other Appledore maids, to bathe; but a wave came up and carried her off, and his little sweetheart was drowned.

And Bill said "he was like one mazed;" that for three days and nights he never left the boat nor took food, for he was up and down the river from Bideford to the Bar, looking for his little sweetheart. On the night of the third day he was out by the Bar; the moon shone down on the long line of white waves. Bill stood up in his boat, and watched the waves flash wild and white in the moonlight; and he cried for his little sweetheart.

Then Bill saw that they were not waves at all, but thousands of beautiful dancing maidens. They all stood in a line, clasping each other's hands. A beautiful living line of fair white dancing maidens reaching across the river from Northern Burrows to Saunton Sands; and in the middle, laughing and tossing her white arms above her head, Bill saw his little sweetheart.

"Bill!" she cried, "I am so happy, dear! Do not seek for me any more, Bill! And do not cry, for I am a mermaid now, and will sing and dance forever, until we meet again, dear Bill."

Then all the mermaids began to sing; and Bill sat and listened, and high above them all he heard his little sweetheart's voice.

Bill never heard or dreamed of such music; the very stars rang with it. But the moon went down, the stars went out, the mermaids hushed their singing and sank beneath the Bar. In the cold grey morning light Bill drifted back to Appledore.

This was the story the Boy loved best of all. His one dream and his one great longing was to see the mermaids.

"Bill," he would say, "do you think you will ever see your little mermaid sweetheart again?"

"By and by," Bill would say. "By and by, maybe, when the Lord pleases."

"Bill, will you take me to the Bar by moonlight?"

But Bill would shake his head, and say, "No, he did not go out at nights now. It was bad for the rheumatics."

So this is what the Appledore Boy did.

The moon was hanging like a silver lamp in the sky when he crept out of his little cot in Betsy's room, put on his little clothes as best he might, lifted the latch of Betsy's door (for she seldom locked it), and stepped out upon the moonlit quay.

There was old Bill's boat rocking softly in the shadows, and loosely tied by a rope to an iron ring in the stonework of the quay. The Boy caught the rope, and pulled the boat towards him; then, slipping in, he pushed her out, and down they went with the tide.

Swiftly and quickly the current took him; swiftly and quickly. The moonlit quay was soon far behind, and he was even with the bright lighthouse light. But the Boy hardly saw it; hardly noticed it gleaming like a fiery rippling pathway to the sand-hills. He was listening; straining every nerve to catch the singing of the mermaidens. But he only heard the thunder of the Bar.

Swifter and swifter the boat went on; and the Boy saw the great white wall of the Bar gleaming and flashing in the moonlight.

The boat began to dance up and down. The Boy stood up, and the salt foam flew in his face.

Ah, yes! ah, yes! he saw them now.

There they all were, dancing and flinging their white arms above their heads, laughing in the moonlight; and then they sang.

The Boy in the boat forgot everything in the world but the mermaids and their song.

"Mermaidens, mermaidens, teach me your song!"

"Boy, come with us and learn it," they cried.

A fair white maiden held out her wet arms to him. "Come," she whispered, "come with me, my beautiful Boy." Was it in his dreams he had heard that sweet low voice? was it in his dreams he had gazed into those wonderful eyes? Ah, well, he could not remember. But he bent to the sweet white maiden, and she took him in her arms. Then she danced with him, and rocked him to and fro, so gently, and sang so sadly and softly, that the Boy fell asleep, and knew no more.

The moon went down. The stars went out. The mermaids hushed their singing, and sank behind the Bar.

The old ferryboat drifted up the misty river in the cold grey morning light; sad, and weary, *and all alone.*

THE SHADOWY HILLSIDE

From *The Rainbow Garden*, 1901.

THE boy lived with his grandfather in the cottage under the moor, where the brown trout-stream hurries past, and the grasses grow long, and tall, and wet.

The boy loved Autumn better than anything else. Yes, even better than his old grandfather. It was Autumn then, so he was very happy.

Behind the cottage the moors sloped up, rich with brown bracken, golden gorse, and purple heather. There the rabbits played in dozens all the day, while the hare would sit with his ears well cocked, wondering why they were all so silly. But it is no good his wondering, for he will never find out.

And it was on this same hillside that the boy so loved to lie,

'The People called it Lonely', by Gratiana Chanter, from *The Rainbow Garden.*

watching the red hawks hovering above him against the blue of the sky, waiting to pounce as they always were on the silly bunnies below. But this the boy never let them do, for he was fond of the rabbits, in spite of their silly ways.

It was a very little cottage where the boy and his grandfather lived. The people called it a lonely cottage, but the grandfather loved it, you see, and so did the boy, and of course the lichens and moss that grew on it must have loved it too, for they clung so closely to it. However, I don't think the people really knew much about the cottage, for they seldom went there.

But why, do you say, did the boy love the Autumn better than anything else he knew?

Well, I never could quite tell. But I think partly because she was so sad and beautiful, and so wonderfully dressed, and, most of all, that she also loved the boy.

One day, while he was lying on the moor behind the cottage, he saw her coming down the valley. At first he thought it was but a whiff of the blue peat smoke which the breeze had carried lightly up the valley and left behind him. But as she came slowly onwards he saw the colour of her glorious hair, as of ripe nuts and the red moor fern, and he caught the light of her dazzling eyes as the flash of a brook under a blue sky. Her floating garments were as the opal mists of the moorland, while her hands were full of crimson rowan berries, and others hung amidst the shadows of her hair.

Nearer and nearer she came, while the boy's heart beat so that he could hardly bear it. Nearer and nearer, till at last she stood still, close behind him with her wonderful eyes.

"Child, why do you love me so?" she asked.

But the boy lay low in the bracken, and hid his face and wept.

And as he wept the mists of her robes went floating, floating, and her eyes grew sadder and sadder.

Then she bent and kissed him, and the touch of her lips seemed as the chilly mists of evening, and the brush of her hair as the falling of autumn leaves.

And every day after this the boy went up on the moor to look for her. The early frost came and trimmed the ground with silver, the leaves in the valley below fell faster, the brown moor fern lay low, and the gossamer and spiders' webs were like filigree.

Ah! but this was a sad time for the old grandfather. For the boy longed so for the beautiful autumn, that he was going away with her on a very long journey, such a long journey that both he and the grandfather knew that he would never come back.

So the grandfather was sad.

Every day the boy crept more slowly up the hill, the bracken was drooping and rotten; the frost did not thaw all day.

The day he went away he crawled once more up the steep hillside. The scent of the peat smoke came sweetly to him, and the murmur of the stream rang faintly far below, when the autumn stood beside him, stood and called him.

And as he looked up and saw her there, her opal robes went floating, floating, weaving strange pictures as they moved; for her hair seemed as showers of golden beech leaves, and her eyes as frosty flowers, all sad and glistening. Her hands still clasped the rowan berry stalks, but the berries had all fallen.

And bending over the boy she took him in her arms, and they went away together.

So the poor old grandfather, the shadowy hillside, and the cottage, were left all alone.

THE FORTY THIEVES OF EXMOOR;
OR, THE DOONES OF BADGWORTHY
The Author's Childhood in the Doone Valley, and Traditions Told Her

Auckland Star, 21 April 1894, p. 3.

The first thing that I can remember of the valley where the Doones once lived, was long ago when I was quite a little girl, and sat building a castle out of the ruins of the very houses they once lived in. Those poor tumbled-down ruins which had once been the stronghold and the hiding place of the terrible 'Doones of Badgworthy!'

I remember how angry the furze-chats were, because they thought I was hunting for their nests.[51] They sat on the sharp points of the yellow furze, and scolded at me, but I did not mind them a bit. I only thought how pretty they were; what bright eyes they had, and what a way they had of making a fuss about nothing. For I did not want their nest just then; I wanted to build my castle.

And then I remember how I took up a big grey stone, and under it hurried and skurried and flurried, a whole colony of red ants. I remember how I laughed to see them tumble over one another, and drag their fat white eggs into little holes and tiny tunnels and weeny underground passages. I felt quite proud to have caused such a commotion in the little world, and wondered where the passages led to, and if there were any rooms below. So I poked with a bit of stick to see. But the soft earth passages fell in and buried the ants, and I felt ashamed of having teased them so. Then

---

[51] Furze-chat: stonechat (a small chat, a little smaller than a robin).

an ant bit me on the hand, so I went away to get another stone for my castle, and left the ants to build theirs up again.

Under this stone I found something else. What do you think? Well, a family of young snakes. You may fancy how quickly I dropped the stone, and how fast I ran away. The snakes were a beautiful red brown colour, and wriggled delightfully. Still, I knew an adder by sight, and I knew he could bite—so I ran away.

Somehow, my castle did not get on so well after that. I had an uncomfortable feeling that there were snakes under every stone—and I quite believe there were under a great many. So I sat down a bit, and watched a skylark go up and up into the sky, and a red hawk hover. He was watching some poor little bunny or mouse that he wanted for his supper, and I did wish he wouldn't get it. Of a sudden he swooped. I turned round quickly to see where he had gone and toppled right over the bank of the Doones' house into a bed of nettles.

'Come, baby,' said my sister, 'let us find a dockleaf.'

Then I believe I cried, for the nettles hurt a good deal.

But that was long ago, and when I grew bigger people told me wonderful and wild stories about the same Doone Valley, where I had built my castle—stories of Forty Thieves—the terrible Doones of Badgworthy.

They told me a great treasure was buried in that same valley—gold and jewels, which the lawless Doones had taken from terrified people in coaches and carriages on the highroads. And other lovely things they had stolen from time to time—they were all buried somewhere, deep down, where no one should find them. For many folks had dug and dug, from rise of sun, until the long shadows spread over the lonely Doone Glen, but never as yet had they found the treasure of the Doones.

One man discovered a passage which led under the ground. He followed it in, and every step he took he thought was bringing him nearer to the hidden treasure. But suddenly he was brought to a standstill. He could go no farther. The passage had fallen in—even as the ants' had—and he groped his way back again into the daylight, terribly disappointed, and maybe leaving the treasure behind him. If it is there, it is buried deep and still remains to be found.

Then they told me that there was a gun in the old farmhouse on the hill; an old gun which the farmer treasured, for one of the last Doones was shot with it, and a woman had shot him.

Now, before I go any further with my story about the Doones and their evil doings, let me tell you what Exmoor is like, as far as I can in a few words, so that you may understand how difficult it was for the people to hunt down these lawless robbers, and how easy it was for them to get away.

There are miles and miles of wide open moorland—hills and valleys, valleys and hills, the whole way round as far as you can see. All the rounded hills are covered with brown heather in the winter and purple in the summer. Every valley has its tumbling trout stream full of trout—of which I have caught many a good basketful. Some of the valleys have thick oak woods, where the great red deer lie. There are deep black bogs, on the moor, which will swallow a man and horse, if they are unlucky enough to get into them.

It is a beautiful wild country to wander over, on a summer's day, or evening, when the sun glows over the purple moors, and the air is full of the scent of the heather, the singing of larks and the humming of bees. But it is a different matter on a stormy night or in a blinding fog, for the moor is the land of marsh and fog. People often get lost on moors, when the fog comes down like a white wet blanket—even those who know it the best.

You may wander on the moor for whole days, and never meet a human being—only wild birds, wild deer and wild ponies.

Here, in a lonely glen, surrounded by open heath-covered moors, and within easy distance of the farms which they robbed when they liked, the terrible Doones took up their abode. There they built their houses and the great ovens in which they baked their bread—bread made of the flour they had stolen from the farmers on their way to market. You can still see the ruins of the great ovens, the stones are covered with white and yellow lichens, nettles grow inside, and never more will bread be baked in the oven of the Doones.

The other night old Bate came to see me—not the old god of the heathens, though for all I know he may have got his name from him.[52]

Surely, though, he is a son of Anak!—for he is a grand old giant, with vast shoulders, blue eyes, and hair as silver as the gleam of moonlight on his own moorland streams.

Bate's father was on Nelson's ship, when Nelson died. He had seen the beautiful Lady Hamilton. He had seen Caracciolo hang from the yardarm of the ship.[53] He had helped to tie 40 pounds of shot to his head and his heels, and seen the corpse float after!—so that they rowed him ashore after all, and buried him on dry land. But I must tell you no more of Bate's father, though his adventures were most interesting, and would fill a book, but of Bate himself, and what he told me about the Doones.

---

52 Bate: John Bate of Tippacott, see Frederick John Snell, *The Blackmore Country*. London: Adam and Charles Black, 1906, p. 151.

53 Francesco Caracciolo, who was charged with high treason and hanged from the yard-arm of the *Minerva*.

'Fifty years agone,' he said, 'I used to go sheepherding in the Doone Valley, and father, well, he did the same before me, until he runned away to sea. But, bless 'ee! I know every stick and stone out over the moor, and if I don't, who should!

'Father told me; and his father told he before him that the Doone come from a place called Northumberland, a good ways off from here. There'd been a rebellion up here, he said. And they'd got turned out of the country. So they runned away to Exmoor, being a wildish sort of place, where they couldn't easily be tracked.

'There was an old farmhouse in the Doone Valley. I can mind it myself, for I helped to pull it down, nigh 40 year agone. 'Twas a quar old place, to be sure; however it come to be built in such an outlandish spot I can't tell'ee. 'Twas a terrible pity to pull it down. For 'twas an old-fashioned place; full of queer passages, and odd rooms. Well built, too; though 'twas so many years agone. Well, this old house, I heard father say, was built long before the Doones comed there.

' 'Twas one terrible snowy night, when the wind was blowing fierce out over the Black Hills that the Doones first found their way to Badgworthy Water. An old farmer and his maid were in the house. But the Doones they turned him right out neck and heel—though 'twas a night that no one but a Doone would have turned a dog out in. Well, I've heard my father say, they was both picked up dead, stone dead. The maid up by the withybush, and the man farther in over the forest.[54] I reckon the snow and the Doones between them, had done for them, sure enough, poor souls!

'I've heard father say, that the Doones was respectable farmers in their own country, and farmed their own land. But they never

54 Withybush: willow bush.

tilled a bit in Badgworthy Bottom and took to thriving wonderful quick. Everything they wanted they helped themselves to, sheep, cows, pigs, corn, hay and horses. Even some of the women and children round was carried off. The farmers could do nought, for they was so few and the Doones so many. They was terrible folk to be sure.

'There must have been ten families altogether, and forty men. So father's father told him. But they didn't all settle there at once, but came in twos and threes. No doubt but what they found it an easy thing to live by other men's toil. And that Exmoor mutton was sweet.

'Father said they'd shoot any man who had got a word to say to him. So 'twas best to bide quiet.

'Once, so he said, the Doones had been off Winehead way robbing a farmhouse. They got all they wanted, and was coming home again, when someone fired at them in the dark. No person said he was hurt, so they rode right on and took no account of it.

'They had ridden some miles over the heather, when one of their men fell from his saddle, dead! The Doones they laid him right down in the heath, and rode straight back to the village where the shot was fired. And father said he heard tell that there was not one soul left alive but one little maid, who was quite mazed with all the terrible sights she'd a seed.

'Yes, the folks round was terribly afeared of them, and well they might be.

'But I fancy, from what father said, that it got so bad at last that the Government interfered. But I haint quite sure, for they didn't take much account of these parts in those days; and things went on, I fancy, pretty much as they liked.

'But I know in time the farmers got pretty mad, and shot the

Doones down like snipe, whenever they got the chance. They say that one of them was shot to Robber's Bridge to Dareford—and that's why 'tis called Robber's Bridge. That another was shot out of the window up to Yanworthy by the farmer's wife.

'She was left all alone, poor soul! Her husband had gone to Porlock market, and was not coming back that night. She was in bed when she heard someone shouting to her to come down and unbar the door. She looked out of the window and saw a great tall man standing in the moonlight. She knew in a minute, 'twas a Doone. She took her husband's loaded gun from the corner, opened the window and shot him dead. There was only one; lucky for her; but she finished that one. They've got that gun now, hung up to the ceiling of Yanworthy kitchen. I dare say you've a seed it, miss?'

Why yes! I had seen it often—always slung up to the old oak beams in the kitchen at Yanworthy. It is a long slim gun, so old they are almost afraid to take it down for fear it will crumble to pieces, but still kept and treasured in memory of a darling deed!

And still the sun shines on the lonely valley of the Doones. The rain beats, and the wind howls. The savage Doones are all dead, years and years ago. But the story of their bloody deeds is yet told by the country folk. And the old gun still hangs to the smoke stained rafters at Yanworthy, telling its tale of lawless days and desperate times. Those few grey stones at the bottom of the glen, where I played as a child, are all that is left of the once feared and famous stronghold. And only the ants and snakes know where to find the hidden treasure of the terrible Doones of Badgworthy.

GLOSSARY

Some of the words and phrases listed below have multiple meanings. The translations given here are accurate for their use within this volume only.

B'aint: ain't
Besom: a broom made from thin twigs.
Bide: stay, remain.
Blunk: a flake of snow.
Chiel: child.
Clackering: clattering
Cleve: a cliff, the steep side of a hill.
Combe: a steep, short valley running up from the sea.
Cream: go pale.
Dimpsey: twilight, also dim or dark.
Dips: dip-candles.
Flitter: flutter.
Fuzz: furze, gorse.
Fye: *lit.* 'faith', used as an assertion or quasi-oath, meaning 'by my faith', 'verily' or 'truly'.
Glidder: frosted, slippery.
Heath: heather.
Iss: yes.
Iss fye: l*it.* 'yes faith', used as an assertion or quasi-oath, meaning 'yes, by my faith', 'yes, verily' or 'yes, truly'.
Mazed: mad, daft, stupid.
Mind: remember.

Mopesing: moping.
Peart: cheerful, lively.
Pixy's stools: toadstools, mushrooms.
Pummel-footed: club-footed or clumsy.
Saith: said.
Scat: *noun* fig, *verb* scattered.
Sloans: Sloe berries, from the *Prunus spinosa.*
Smitch: smoke.
Snack: a sneer or cutting remark.
Study: consider, care for.
Suent: pleasant, agreeable, kindly.
Tay: tea.
Telling: talking.
Turf: a block of peat.
Vake: a piece of business.
Wanged away: yielded to exhaustion, faded away.
Whirlfooted: club-footed.
Widdle: a cape or shawl.
Windhover: a kestrel.
Wist: haunted or pixie-led (a place where you are likely to be led astray by pixies).
Withys: willows.
Woolpacks: masses of fleecy white clouds.
Worrit: worry.
Zimmed: thought.